Hannah and the
Daring Escape

Best Friends

#12

Hannah and the Daring Escape

Hilda Stahl

CROSSWAY BOOKS • WHEATON, ILLINOIS
A DIVISION OF GOOD NEWS PUBLISHERS

Hannah and the Daring Escape.

Copyright © 1993 by Word Spinners, Inc.

Published by Crossway Books
        a division of
        Good News Publishers
        1300 Crescent Street
        Wheaton, Illinois 60187.

Cover illustration: Paul Casale

Art Direction/Design: Mark Schramm

First printing, 1993

Printed in the United States of America

Library of Congress Cataloging-in-Publication Data
Stahl, Hilda.
    Hannah's and the daring escape / Hilda Stahl.
      p.   cm. — (Best Friends ; #12)
    Summary: While attending a special art class, twelve-year-old Hannah Shigwam, one of the King's Kids, helps a frightened classmate who is certain that someone is after her.
    [1. Christian life—Fiction.   2. Mystery and detective stories.
3. Artists—Fiction.] I. Title. II. Series: Stahl, Hilda.
Best Friends ; #12.
PZ7.S78244Hap 1993   [Fic]—dc20   92-43994
ISBN 0-89107-714-6

01		00		99		98		97		96		95		94		93
15	14	13	12	11	10	9	8	7	6	5	4	3	2	1

To John Franks

Contents

1

A Beautiful Girl

With her hairbrush in her hand, Hannah Shigwam smiled at her reflection in the restroom mirror at Andrews Art Academy. Was she really beautiful? Yesterday Mr. Jarman had walked right up to her in art class and said, "Hannah, you're a beautiful girl, and you do beautiful work."

Her heart had jerked, but she managed to say, "Thank you."

Today his words still sent her heart hammering wildly. She sometimes felt that people looked down on her because she was Ottawa Indian, but the famous artist thought she was beautiful! He also thought her painting was beautiful! Hannah smiled dreamily. The Best Friends—Chelsea McCrea, Roxie Shoulders, and Kathy Aber—had often told her her work was great, but since they were her friends she expected nice words from them. But Clint Jarman was different. As an artist as well as an art instructor, he wouldn't say her work was good unless it really was. And he wouldn't say she was beautiful if he didn't mean it. He had an eye for beauty.

Again she smiled into the large mirror above the row of white sinks. The mirror shot back her reflection. Her long shiny black hair hung down her back and over her shoulders onto her red sweater. Her black eyes flashed with excitement. For almost two weeks of afternoons after school she'd been in Mr. Jarman's art class here at the academy. Last month when she showed Mom and Dad the information about the class, they immediately agreed she could attend. Mrs. Shoulders, Roxie's mom, offered to drive her back and forth each day because she was working nearby.

"It all worked out sooo well," Hannah whispered.

But everything wasn't perfect, because now the time was almost up, and she'd probably never get to see Clint Jarman again. She sighed heavily. Now the mirror shot back the reflection of a sad twelve-year-old girl. She squared her shoulders, lifted her head, and tried to look ten years older. It didn't help at all. She was twelve, and she'd have to wait ten years to look ten years older.

Just then the bathroom door burst open, and a thin, blonde girl rushed in, her face white and her green eyes wide with fear. She wore baggy gray pants and a loose-fitting black and gray blouse held tight with a wide black belt at her narrow waist. She spotted Hannah and stopped short. She'd obviously hoped the restroom would be empty.

"Hi." Hannah smiled hesitantly. She'd seen the girl in class, but they hadn't spoken. "I'm Hannah Shigwam."

"I'm Penny Graham." She backed toward the door.

Hannah flipped back her dark hair. She had to say something so Penny wouldn't run away in fear. "We're the youngest in our class, aren't we?" Great dialogue! That was sure to make Penny feel at ease!

"I guess so." Penny took another step back. She didn't want to talk to anyone. She didn't dare trust anyone.

Hannah lifted her brows questioningly. "Is something wrong?"

Penny shrugged. Her mouth felt dry. "Should there be?"

"You look . . . frightened."

Penny shivered and clutched her bag. She *was* frightened! Why not tell Hannah? What harm could it do? "I . . . I thought someone was following me."

Hannah's pulse leaped. Did she smell a mystery? Who would've thought she'd come to art classes and run into a mystery? It was too good to be true. She lowered her voice. "Who would be following you?"

"It could've been the security guard."

The excitement drained out of Hannah. "You're probably right. I know security is really tight now that the Griffin painting is here. Maybe they thought you were after it." Hannah laughed, but the laugh died in her throat when she saw the look on Penny's pale face. "Sorry . . . I was just teasing."

"That's all right." Penny relaxed. Maybe it really had been security guards checking on her. She'd been standing close to the painting to study it. They might've thought she appeared suspicious because of the way she'd kept looking over her shoulder. "I saw the painting."

"You did? I bet it's magnificent!" Hannah dropped her brush back into her pack. "I'm going to look at it after class. Imagine having a Griffin on display here!"

"It's worth half a million dollars!"

Hannah gasped. "That's a *lot* of money." She smiled dreamily. "I wonder how it would feel to sell a painting for that much."

Penny shrugged. She'd dreamed of being a famous artist for a long time, but she'd never thought about the money that could bring. Daddy was already rich, and she hadn't thought about making a fortune of her own. She quickly brushed her hair. "We'll be late if we don't hurry."

"We sure don't want to be late." Hannah hurried out the door, her heart racing at the thought of seeing Mr. Jarman again today. Would he tell her she was beautiful again?

Penny stepped hesitantly into the hall and darted a look around. Several people were walking slowly along, studying the pictures lining the hall between the doors. There was no sign of the man who'd followed her. She hurried around two women and followed Hannah. She shivered and gripped her bag. Maybe she was just being paranoid. Why would anyone follow *her*? She wasn't important. She frowned. But Daddy—a U.S. Senator—*was* important, and he'd warned her to be on her guard at all times. He'd even hired a guard once to stay with her when someone had threatened to hurt his family. Was someone after her because of Daddy? She shivered, stepped into the classroom, and almost bumped into Hannah who stood just inside the large room.

Hannah glanced around. Rows of large drawers where they kept their canvases lined the wall under the windows. Easels with high stools near them stood in rows. The paint and turpentine smelled like exotic perfumes. Her heart raced, and tiny shivers ran up and down her spine. Then she saw *him* standing beside his small desk. The chatter of the students faded into the background. He was less than six feet tall and had warm brown eyes and curly brown hair. His jeans were smeared with paint, and his light blue sweatshirt hung loosely on his body. His steps were quiet in his white sneakers as he walked across the front of the room. Hannah sighed dreamily. Attending Andrews Art Academy was a great honor, but having Clint Jarman as a teacher was a greater honor. His work was outstanding. He could easily be a world-famous artist if he wanted, but instead he taught at Andrews and displayed his work in local art shows.

Penny brushed past Hannah, got her canvas, and sat on the high stool at her easel. She frowned at the way Hannah looked at Clint Jarman. How immature to have a crush on the teacher! Didn't Hannah know Mr. Jarman was married?

Just then a movement at the door caught Penny's attention. She glanced at the door, and her heart plunged to her feet. It was the same man she'd seen earlier! He jerked back when he saw her look at him. Who was he? Why was he watching her? Was it because of the Griffin or because of Daddy? She rubbed her icy hands together. How could she stay in class and work knowing he was outside the door watching and waiting?

Hannah glanced at Penny, saw the terrified look on her face, and looked over her shoulder to follow Penny's gaze. No one was in sight outside the door. Frowning thoughtfully, Hannah got her canvas and hurried to her easel. She glanced up just as Clint Jarman looked up from the paper he was reading. He smiled at her, and her legs were suddenly weak. She eased onto the tall stool at her easel. Why couldn't she be mature enough to say something dazzling to him? Other girls in sixth grade could talk to anyone, even good-looking teachers, but her tongue was tied in a million knots.

Slowly Hannah took out her paints and brushes, then peeked at Clint Jarman across the crowded room just as he pushed his fingers into the back pockets of his jeans. Oh, he was sooo good looking!

"Class, I have an important announcement to make." Mr. Jarman waited until everyone was silent and looking at him. "Not only do we have the Griffin on display, but I was able to make arrangements for the man himself to visit."

Hannah gasped as the others cried out in delight.

Mr. Jarman walked away from his desk and closer to the first row of easels. "Ira Griffin will be here in person Sunday afternoon. All the students and the public are invited."

Hannah clasped her hands in her lap, and her heart swelled with anticipation. Maybe the Best Friends would come. Hannah glanced at Penny Graham, caught her eye, and smiled.

Penny smiled. How wonderful that she'd be able to meet the famous Ira Griffin! Then the smile faded. What if Uncle Royce wouldn't let her come?

He seemed to grow stricter every day. He always wanted to know where she was and who she was with. He said he didn't want her going anywhere with the school kids, nor did he want her to bring any of them home with her. He said he wanted to make sure nobody took advantage of her or tried to harm her because of her dad. But she knew it was more than that—she just couldn't figure out what. She pressed her lips tighter and tighter. She'd find a way to come see Ira Griffin Sunday afternoon no matter what. Surely Uncle Royce wouldn't object, would he? And if he did, she'd come anyway. He had no business keeping her away just to prove she had to obey him while she stayed with him and her aunt. If she had a way to reach Daddy by phone, she'd tell him just how terrible it was staying with Uncle Royce and Aunt Peg.

At her easel Hannah perched on her stool and tried to picture meeting the great Ira Griffin. Would he think she had talent? Or would he ignore her because she was Ottawa? She sighed and locked her suddenly icy hands together.

Just then she remembered that Sunday was the special gathering of the Shigwam family—a time when they met to talk about the Ottawas so the young people would know their heritage and be proud of it. Cousin Ginny would be there. Hannah bit her lip. She hadn't seen Ginny since the Fourth of July when Ginny had purposely knocked a paper cup filled with punch on the special dress Great-grandmother had let Hannah wear for the occasion. It was made of fine tanned leather and was covered with beautiful beadwork. It had fringe at the sleeves and around the hem. Ginny had wanted it for herself, but Great-grandmother had given it to Hannah. And Cousin Ansell would be there too. He hadn't gotten together with the family since Hannah's dad had helped him. He was an alcoholic, but he wanted help, and Dad had gladly done all he could. He said he was all for the mentor program Native Americans had established. Would Dad give up the afternoon to bring her to see Mr. Griffin?

Hannah forced her attention on what Mr. Jarman was saying about today's work. Tonight she'd talk to Mom and Dad. They just had to let her come Sunday!

2

Best Friends

Hannah swallowed her bite of pizza. She couldn't wait to tell the Best Friends the exciting news about Ira Griffin and the possible mystery with Penny Graham! She'd met Chelsea, Roxie, and Kathy at Pizza Palace in the mall a few minutes earlier. She sat in the booth beside Chelsea and across from Roxie and Kathy. The other girls had already ordered and started eating before Hannah got there. Talking, laughter, and the clink of silverware filled the tiny restaurant. The aroma of baking pizza wove in and out of the smells of garlic bread and people. Chelsea was in the middle of a story about Joan Golnek. Even in the dimly lit restaurant Chelsea's hair looked bright red. It was harder to see the freckles that covered her though. She had been Hannah's very first friend. They'd met in the spring when Chelsea and her family had moved from Oklahoma to Middle Lake, Michigan, into the subdivision, The Ravines—right across the street from Hannah.

"Teaching Joan photography sure is fun!" Chelsea took a drink, then set her glass of ice water in place. She pushed the sleeves of her blue sweater up her freckled arms. "I thought it would be boring, but she's good! When she joins the Photography Club and enters her work in competition, she'll win all the ribbons. I mean it!"

Roxie wiped pizza sauce off her lips. She wore a yellow sweater that made her wide brown eyes and short brown hair seem even darker. "I couldn't believe it, but I saw her and Kesha Bronski eating together at school today."

"They're friends!" Chelsea's eyes sparkled happily. "They both needed a friend, and they found each other."

"I think that's great." Kathy reached for another piece of pizza. The cheese stretched all the way from the pan in the center of the small table to her white plate. Kathy had natural curly blonde hair that she'd trade any day for beautiful straight blonde hair she could comb easily. Sometimes she couldn't even get a pick through her hair. Kathy giggled. "Treva Joerger doesn't like it a bit that they're friends! I thought she'd scream when she saw them. But she didn't."

Roxie nodded. "Treva's been sooo nice since we told everybody she and Joan are cousins."

HILDA STAHL

"Treva sure didn't want anybody to know," Kathy added. "She's really a snob."

Hannah couldn't hold back her news a second longer. "You wouldn't believe who's going to be at Andrews Art Academy." She waited for the others to turn to her to hear her news, but they didn't. They were looking at the door. She frowned. Why were they looking at the woman walking in? She was ordinary looking. "What?" she finally asked.

Chelsea leaned close to Hannah and whispered, "That's Susan Conners. She hired us today to decorate her Christmas tree. She wants us there Saturday morning at 10."

Hannah frowned. "Oh." That news was nothing compared to hers. "Well, let me tell you about today . . ."

Roxie leaned forward. "I never knew anyone who hired somebody to decorate their tree. Have you?"

"No." Kathy nudged Chelsea. "Do we get to decorate the way we want?"

"I don't know."

"I hope we can." Roxie lifted her pizza to her mouth. "I wouldn't want Mrs. Conners to tell us how to do it."

Hannah tapped her spoon against her glass. The sound filled the space around them, and she laughed. The Best Friends looked at her questioningly. "I have news."

"You do?"

"What is it?"

"Why didn't you tell us?"

Hannah rolled her eyes. "You didn't give me a chance." As quickly as she could, she told them about Ira Griffin. "Will you go see the Griffin with me? If I get to go, I mean."

"Sure!" they all said at once.

"Great!" Hannah took a deep breath. "There's more." She was almost bursting with it. She quickly told them about Penny.

"Will we meet Penny on Sunday?" Roxie asked.

"If she's there. She was really afraid of someone. It could've been the security guard though." Hannah frowned thoughtfully. "But then again it could be something else."

The others laughed. Roxie said, "Hannah, you're always looking for a mystery."

Hannah shrugged. "I just like to solve mysteries."

"We know," they all said together, then giggled.

Hannah giggled with them. She bit into the pizza while they talked about other things. She thought about telling them Mr. Jarman had said she was beautiful, but for some reason she couldn't talk about it even to them.

During a lull in the conversation Chelsea said, "I think we should decide what we want to do for

Christmas. Draw names? Buy gifts for all of us? What?"

Kathy laughed. "Is this a Best Friends Club meeting?"

"Or a *King's Kids* meeting?" Roxie chuckled.

Hannah laughed with them. It seemed like each time they got together Chelsea had to take care of some business. None of them objected, but it was really funny. They thought it was because Chelsea was such an organizer. She'd started the *King's Kids* business venture with the motto "Great or small, we do it all." They did odd jobs around the neighborhood. In the summer they'd all worked a lot, but during school they'd voted to work only once or twice a week.

Chelsea shrugged. "Christmas is coming fast, girls. We don't want to wait until the last minute to know what we're going to do. Draw names or what?"

"Draw names," Hannah and Roxie said at the same time.

"Buy for everyone," Kathy said, then she shrugged. "It really doesn't matter to me. Just so we have a sleepover and make chocolate-chip cookies and play games."

An idea popped into Hannah's head. "I have it! This is sooo great you'll all vote to do it!"

"What?" They all looked at Hannah expectantly.

"We'll find a family who really needs gifts, and we'll buy for them instead of for each other!" Hannah's eyes sparkled as she waited for their reaction. They didn't say anything for a long time. Her stomach knotted. Had it been a dumb idea? She turned to Chelsea. "So . . . what do you think?"

Chelsea slowly nodded. "I like it. But how will we find a family in need?"

"Easy." Hannah pushed back her plate. "My dad will know one. He always does."

"Let's take a vote." Chelsea looked at each one. "Is it yes or no?"

"Yes!" they all said.

Hannah sighed in relief. "I was afraid you hated my idea."

Roxie wrinkled her nose. "Sometimes you're so nice it scares me. *I* am never that nice!"

"You're learning," Kathy said softly. "We're all trying to be like Jesus."

Chelsea nudged Hannah with her elbow. "Since we're having a meeting, did you remember you're supposed to have the Scripture for the day?" They always shared a verse from the Bible at their meetings.

Hannah laughed. "I thought I'd have a chance to go home first before the meeting. I have it written on a scrap of paper on my dresser."

"Try to remember it."

Hannah thought for a minute, but shook her

head. "I do remember Psalm 119:11. 'Your word have I hid in my heart, that I might not sin against you.'"

"That's a good one," Chelsea said softly.

Smiling, Hannah nodded.

Later at home Hannah walked slowly downstairs where she shared the entire basement as a bedroom/playroom with her three little sisters—Sherry, Vivian, and Lena. Lena was already there. She jumped guiltily away from the dresser the twins shared.

"What're you doing?" Hannah asked sharply.

"Nothing." Lena dropped to the edge of her bed and rubbed her hands down her jeans. A red ribbon held her black hair back.

"I saw you." Hannah dropped her bag on the bed and faced Lena again. The beds were neatly made with matching spreads. Toys were scattered in the corner where the twins had their toys. Hannah frowned. "Are you snooping in the twins' things again?"

Lena looked ready to cry. "They said they took something of mine."

Hannah hung her jacket in the closet that stretched across one entire wall. All four of them shared it, and there was still room left over. Hannah tried to think of something helpful to say to Lena. Sometimes at twelve it was very hard to be the oldest in the family. Lena was nine and the twins eight.

Baby Burke was old enough to sit by himself and spit out his babyfood when he didn't like it. Hannah faced Lena. "What's the problem this time?" Often the twins didn't include Lena in their plans.

Lena brushed a tear off her cheek. "Heather Robbins wants to start a Best Friends Club. She asked the twins but not me. I thought she was going to ask me."

"So did I." Hannah hooked her hair behind her ears as she walked across the room. "She told me so when I talked to her the other day."

"The twins said she didn't invite me." Lena twisted the bottom of her sweater around her hand. "I was trying to find the note Heather wrote to them."

"Why not call Heather?"

"No way!" Lena shook her head so hard, her shoulder-length black hair whipped across her face. "What if she doesn't want me and tells me so? That would be terrible!" Giant tears filled Lena's eyes. "I've been praying forever for a friend!"

"I know." Hannah slipped her arm around Lena. "Call Heather and tell her you want to be friends with her. It'll give her a chance to tell you about being in her Best Friends Club."

"If she doesn't, I might cry." Lena shivered. "I don't want her to know I'm crying."

"I've seen *her* cry."

"She'll think I'm a baby!"

Hannah pulled Lena close. "You're not a baby. People cry when they get hurt—even adults."

"Not me." Lena sniffed hard and knuckled at her eyes. "What'll I do if she doesn't want me for a friend?" Lena's voice rose in a wail.

"You'll keep trusting God to send you a friend." Hannah jumped up and pulled Lena with her. "Run upstairs and call Heather right now. You can do it!"

"I wish we had a phone in our bedroom, don't you?"

"It doesn't matter."

"Chelsea McCrea has one in her bedroom. Doesn't that make you want one too?"

"No."

Lena looked down at the floor. "If I tell you something, will you hate me?"

"Of course not."

"Sometimes I get jealous when somebody has something I don't have." Lena trembled. "Sometimes I get so jealous, I want to rip Chelsea's phone out of her bedroom and throw it away."

Hannah lifted Lena's face up so she could look into her eyes. "When you start to feel jealous, pray a special blessing on the person you're jealous of. Pray that God will give her the desires of her heart and that more good things will come to her."

Lena gasped. "But I'd be even more jealous then!"

Smiling, Hannah shook her head. "No. Just the opposite. Jesus will take your jealousy right away, and you'll be full of love. Jesus said to seek His kingdom first, and then He'll give you special blessings. When you pray for others, you're doing what Jesus wants you to do. When you do that, He can meet your needs."

Lena hugged Hannah hard. "Thank you! I'm glad you're my sister!"

Hannah laughed. "I hope you remember that when I make you mad."

"I will!" Lena ran for the stairs. "I'll call Heather right now."

"Let me know what she says."

"I will." Lena closed the door with a snap.

"Heavenly Father, thank You for a friend for Lena," Hannah whispered.

Later Hannah walked upstairs. She smelled popcorn and heard the *pop pop pop* of the popcorn maker. She hurried to the kitchen. Dad stood at the counter watching the white kernels land in the bowl. He dribbled melted margarine over it. He'd changed into his old jeans, cowboy boots, and flannel western shirt that snapped up the front. Mom sat at the table feeding Burke cereal in his highchair before he went to bed for the night. Mom was trying everything she could think of to get Burke to sleep the entire night.

"Hi," Hannah said over the noise of the popper and Burke's jabbering.

"Popcorn will be ready in a minute if you want some," Dad said with a wide grin. His name was Burke, but from the time he was in school people had called him Chief. Now everyone did. It didn't bother him at all like it would've some in his family.

Hannah lifted the bowls they always used for popcorn from the cupboard and set them beside the large bowl of white popcorn. "I need to ask you about Sunday."

"Go ahead," Mom said as she pushed another bite into baby Burke's mouth.

Hannah glanced at Dad, and he nodded. Quickly she told them about Ira Griffin and the painting. "So, can we go?"

"I don't know," Mom said, looking questioningly at Dad.

He shrugged. "Sure, we can. This is too important to you to miss. We'll leave the family gathering early."

"Thanks, Dad!" Hannah threw her arms around him and hugged him hard. She should've known he'd agree to going.

"I read something about Ira Griffin just lately." Mom frowned in thought. "Maybe he's not going to paint any longer."

Hannah gasped. "That can't be!"

"I could be wrong." Mom pushed another bite

of cereal into Burke's mouth. He spit it out, and she quickly caught it with the spoon and pushed it right back in.

"I'm sure you are." Hannah couldn't imagine a great artist like Ira Griffin quitting.

Dad dipped a small empty bowl into the large bowl and filled it with popcorn. He held it out to Hannah.

"No thanks, Dad." Slowly Hannah walked out of the kitchen and into the living room where the twins were watching a video. What if Mom were right? Hannah sank weakly to the couch. Maybe she could call Mr. Jarman and ask him.

Her heart leaped, and she flushed. She couldn't call Mr. Jarman. Tomorrow she'd see him at art class, and she could ask him then. It would be terrible if Ira Griffin quit painting.

Just then Lena ran into the room, her eyes sparkling and a big smile on her face. "She said yes!"

Hannah laughed softly. "Good." She pushed thoughts of Ira Griffin away as she listened to Lena.

3

On the Run

Penny Graham ducked into the lounge at Andrews Art Academy and bumped into Hannah Shigwam—again. Her face as white as her blouse, Penny squealed with fright and jumped back.

Hannah reached out to keep Penny from falling. "What's wrong?"

Penny swallowed hard and fought to regain her composure. "He followed me again today," she said hoarsely. Her hand trembling, she pushed her honey-gold hair out of her oval face. Tears sparkled in her green eyes. "I saw him just outside the academy, and I know it was the same man!"

Hannah gently led Penny to the brown sofa. Hannah wanted to get to class and see Clint Jarman, but she couldn't leave Penny when she was so frightened. "Maybe we should report it to the security guard." Hannah sighed. "Maybe that man is a security guard in plain clothes."

Penny sank to the sofa and dropped her bag onto the carpet beside her. She rubbed her hands down her jeans. Snow swirled outside the window. The aroma of the fresh coffee in the coffeemaker across the room filled the air. She looked up at Hannah. "The man wore brown dress pants and a thick brown sweater. I guess he could be security undercover." But in her heart she didn't believe it.

Shivers ran up and down Hannah's spine. "Why would anyone follow you?"

Penny shrugged. She couldn't tell Hannah what she suspected.

Hannah moved restlessly. "Did you tell your parents?"

"They're in Europe and won't be back until just before Christmas." A tear slipped down Penny's cheek and splashed onto the back of her hand. "I'm staying with my aunt and uncle."

Hannah suddenly felt too hot. She slipped off her jacket. "Did you tell them?"

"No!" Penny shook her head hard. "I could never never tell Uncle Royce or Aunt Peg!"

"Why not?"

Penny twisted a strand of hair around her finger. Could she trust Hannah? What harm would it do to confide in her? "You might not believe me."

Hannah locked her hands in her lap. "Tell me anyway."

Penny hooked her hair behind her ears. She

didn't say anything for a long time. "My uncle hates me! I don't know why, but he does."

Hannah shivered. "Then why do you stay with him?"

"Daddy said to."

"Why'd your uncle agree?"

Penny pushed the sleeves of her sweater up her arms. "He and Daddy were in a fight for years and just last year they made up. So, I didn't want to tell Daddy I wouldn't stay with Uncle Royce." Penny trembled. "Now I wish I had!" She took another deep breath. "He said he wanted to keep me so Daddy wouldn't think he was still angry."

Hannah watched the snow swirl at the window as her brain whirled with thoughts. Finally she turned back to Penny. "Maybe your uncle is having you followed for some reason."

"I can't think why he would. There must be some other explanation. Daddy is an important man in politics, and he's told me to be careful so some weird person doesn't hurt me." Penny pressed her hand to her throat. "I don't know what to do!"

"God watches over you," Hannah said softly.

Penny took a deep breath. "I know. I guess sometimes I forget."

Hannah glanced toward the lounge door. "Has the man who's been following you tried to stop you or force you to go with him?"

"No. He just follows me. It's awful!" Penny shivered.

Hannah jumped up and started for the door. "Let's go talk to the school security."

"No!" Penny leaped up and caught Hannah's arm. "What if it's only my imagination? Daddy says I'm a creative person with a wild imagination. Once last year I thought an old man was waiting to grab me, so we called the police. It turned out the man stood in the same place every day to catch a ride. I was really really embarrassed. I don't want that to happen again."

Hannah frowned. "Then what'll you do?"

"I wish I knew!"

Hannah looked out the door. Students, laughing and talking, were hurrying to the classrooms. "If the man is really after you, he could hurt you and no one would know."

Penny shivered again.

Hannah turned to face Penny. "Mrs. Shoulders is picking me up after class. We'll talk to her. She might know what to do."

Penny shook her head. "No . . . No . . . I don't want to tell anyone!" It had to be her imagination. Why would anyone follow her without grabbing her? "If the man is following me, maybe it's to protect me."

"Then ask him!" Hannah said sharply.

"I just can't," Penny whispered. She forced a

laugh. "I'm all right. Really. Thanks for listening. I do feel better. You're the only person from the art class who has spoken to me."

"I guess they all think we're too young to bother with."

"Mr. Jarman talks to me, of course."

Hannah smiled dreamily. "He's great, isn't he?"

Penny frowned impatiently. "He's married."

"He is?"

"I met his wife a few days ago when I first came. She's not an artist."

"What is she?"

"A teacher. A reading teacher where I go to school."

Hannah stood very still. "Is she beautiful?"

"I guess. She could be if she dressed differently. She sometimes looks upset and tired in school."

Hannah glanced out into the hall. A woman walked past, her high heels clicking loudly on the tile floor. Mr. Jarman was married! But of course he would be. She should've realized. Tears burned her eyes, and she forced them away. "We better get to class before we're late. I'll go out first and see if the man is there."

"Thanks." Penny bit her bottom lip and waited for Hannah to check the hall.

She looked all around for the man Penny had described. The man wasn't in sight. Hannah motioned to Penny. "It's clear."

Shivering, Penny gripped her pack and hurried after Hannah. Was the man hiding inside a classroom, waiting for a chance to grab her?

Hannah stopped in the classroom doorway and waited for Penny. "Are you coming Sunday to hear Ira Griffin?"

Penny nodded.

"My family and best friends are coming. I want them to meet you."

"I don't know . . ." Penny's voice trailed off.

"You'll like them." Hannah smiled. "And they'll like you, I know."

Penny sighed. "I wish my mom and dad were here, so they could come. Daddy likes Ira Griffin's work a lot." They'd all seen his work in a New York gallery. Daddy had tried to buy one, but they were already sold. For some strange reason Mom had been glad. Mom wouldn't look at anything of Ira Griffin's. It was very strange.

Penny managed to smile at Hannah, then hurried to her easel. Maybe if she tried hard enough, she wouldn't think about the man she thought was following her.

Hannah peeked through her lashes at Mr. Jarman. He was married! Her lip trembling, she pulled her canvas from the drawer and walked to her easel.

After class Penny reluctantly followed Hannah to the parking lot where Mrs. Shoulders waited in her station wagon. The snow had stopped, leaving a light blanket over the parking lot and the nearby trees. Tall lights lit the area as bright as daylight. Penny shivered. She usually walked home because the streets were well-lit too, and she enjoyed walking.

Hannah introduced Penny to Mrs. Shoulders. "Do you mind taking Penny home? It's only a couple of blocks from here."

"Not at all." Mrs. Shoulders smiled at Penny. "It's a little nippy to walk."

"I don't mind walking." Penny settled in the backseat and gave Mrs. Shoulders directions. At the curb outside the house Penny said, "Thanks for the ride."

"You're very welcome." Mrs. Shoulders turned the heater down.

Peggy lifted out her pack. "See you Sunday afternoon."

"See you," Hannah said.

With a wave of her hand Penny ran up the driveway and to the front door. She looked over her shoulder as Mrs. Shoulders and Hannah drove away. Penny darted a look around. Could someone be hiding in the shadows of the bushes along the sidewalk? Lights streamed out from the nearby houses. In the distance a siren wailed.

Trembling, Penny quietly unlocked the front door and slipped into the warm house. She was home sooner than usual. Loud angry voices came from the den. Her stomach knotted. Aunt Peg and Uncle Royce fought a lot, and she hated hearing them. She eased the door shut, then just stood there, barely breathing. Aunt Peg stopped yelling as if they were listening. The *whir* of the furnace suddenly seemed extra-loud. Penny bit her lip. Should she let them know she was home or just creep to her room? She couldn't face them tonight—not when they were obviously angry at each other.

Her bag in her hand, she walked silently across the room.

"I won't let you do that to your brother's girl, Royce!" Aunt Peg shouted.

Penny stopped short. Do what?

"Don't pretend to care," Uncle Royce snapped.

Her face ashen, Penny stood rooted to the spot. Icy splinters of fear pricked her skin.

"I thought you and Jason had finally settled your argument," Aunt Peg said sharply.

Royce laughed dryly. "Jason thinks he can do anything since he's such a big shot, but he can't. I won't forgive and forget so easily. And now that I can make some big money because I have Penny here, Jason won't get away with treating me in such a rotten way."

Penny cringed. What could Uncle Royce mean?

"Don't punish Penny for something her father did to you," Aunt Peg said.

"Why not? What hurts her will hurt him worse."

"Royce, don't do anything so cruel!"

"I'll do as I please with her . . . beat her . . . lock her up . . . starve her."

Penny's legs trembled, and she almost sank to the floor. Was he serious? He sounded like it. Frantically she looked around the living room. What should she do? Daddy had given her plenty of money, but Uncle Royce had taken it for safe keeping—or so he'd said. All she had in her bag was four dollars!

"You're not serious, Royce!" Aunt Peg cried.

"I'll do even more than I said," he said harshly.

Penny's stomach cramped painfully. She had to get out! She walked slowly to the front door. Her hand shook as she reached for the door knob. Could she go outdoors into the possible danger there? But staying inside was even more risky. Where could she go? Who'd help her? If she were in Boston, she'd have friends to stay with, but she didn't know anyone here. Hannah's name popped into her head. Of course! She'd call Hannah!

Cautiously Penny opened the door and slipped back outdoors. Icy wind tangled her hair and chilled her to the bone. Where could she go to call Hannah?

"The art academy!" Penny whispered. They had classes until late at night. A sob rose in her throat, but she choked it back. She hoisted the strap of her bag onto her shoulder and ran down the sidewalk, leaving footprints in the fine dusting of snow. Music drifted from a house she passed. A dog barked.

Several minutes later Penny burst through the heavy glass door at Andrews Art Academy. Heat surrounded her, warming her. The halls were empty. Voices drifted out from a classroom further down the hall. She'd get Hannah's phone number from the office and call her.

Penny ran to the office, stopped at the door, and gasped in alarm. The office was closed!

Voices floated from a classroom, and someone laughed. Heels *tap-tapped* on the tile. Penny glanced around and saw a woman walking down the hall. Trembling, Penny ducked inside the lounge and waited until the footsteps faded away. Slowly she looked around the small room at the couches and chairs. She could hide behind a couch if necessary. The smell of coffee filled the air. A pay phone hung beside the door with a large phone book dangling on a heavy chain. She could look up Hannah's number! She ran to the phone and held the heavy book in her hands. What was Hannah's last name? It was a strange name—one she'd never heard before. She frowned thoughtfully. "It started with a *T*. No, an *S*. Oh, what is it!" No matter how hard she thought, she couldn't remember Hannah's last name.

Frantically Penny flipped through the book,

reading names at random, hoping she'd recall the name if she read it. But she just couldn't remember. Impatiently she slammed the book closed and let it dangle back down. What would she do now?

Nervously she peeked out the door again, then jumped back, her heart thundering in her ears. The man who'd been following her was deep in conversation with another man as they walked slowly down the hall—right toward the lounge!

Frenzied, Penny darted a look around the room for the best hiding-place. The long brown sofa would work the best. She dashed over to it, pushed her bag between the sofa and the wall, and crawled in after it. Dust tickled her nose, and she rubbed it to hold back a sneeze. Awkwardly she pushed the bag where she wanted it, then stretched out on her side, using the bag as her pillow. She was a little shorter than the sofa, so she knew no one could see her unless they looked behind the couch. *Please, please, don't anyone look back here*, she thought to herself. Maybe she'd have to spend the night hidden in the lounge!

She strained to hear sounds outside the lounge. She heard voices but couldn't make out the words. A tear trickled down the side of her face. How could Uncle Royce be so cruel? Somehow she had to get Daddy's itinerary from Uncle Royce and call him to tell him what was happening. But how could she get the itinerary? She needed her money and her clothes too. How could she get them? Maybe tomorrow she could ask Hannah for help.

Penny pressed her hand over her mouth to force back a whimper.

After a million years, when she knew everyone had left, she forced herself to call Uncle Royce. When he answered, she almost dropped the phone.

She closed her eyes and said in as normal a voice as she could manage, "I'm staying with a friend tonight. I won't be home."

"I want you home now!" he shouted. "This instant!"

She trembled so badly, she almost dropped the phone. "Sorry, but I'm staying here. Daddy wouldn't care." It was all she could do to keep from screaming at Uncle Royce.

"You belong here. You come home now or I'll come get you." He sounded angry enough to beat her.

She shivered. "I won't come home!"

"Where are you?" His voice rose until he was shouting. "Penny! Tell me this minute!"

"I'm staying here until I feel like leaving!" She slammed the receiver into place. Tears slipped down her ashen cheeks. Her legs felt too weak to support her. After a long time she walked slowly back to the sofa and slipped behind it just in case.

She lay a long time in the great silence. She shivered and pulled her jacket tight around her. After a long time she heard the guard whistling as he walked the hall. The sound somehow comforted her. She wasn't alone. She closed her eyes and finally drifted off to sleep.

4

The Christmas Tree

Her nose red from the cold wind, Hannah laid her bike beside Chelsea's and ran to Susan Conners's back door. She was late! Chelsea had offered to wait for her, but she'd told her to go on to the job so Mrs. Conners wouldn't be upset. One of the *King's Kids* rules was to be on time. This was the first time Hannah had ever been late. She'd overslept because last night her mind had been full of Penny Graham, Ira Griffin, and, of course, Clint Jarman. She hadn't gone to sleep until after 2, and then she dreamed about Clint Jarman. What a beautiful dream! She smiled, then flushed. It was wrong even to think about loving Mr. Jarman. He was married. And he was as old as Dad! But the thoughts of marrying Mr. Jarman popped into her head anyway. It would be wonderful to be with him all the time and learn everything he knew about art. Maybe she should become an art instructor so they could be together more.

"Stop it, Hannah!" she whispered sharply. It wasn't right to even think about loving and marrying Mr. Jarman.

Sighing, Hannah rang the back doorbell. She heard the melody chime inside. Her breath hung in the cold air, and she moved from foot to foot to try to stay warm.

Chelsea opened the door and smiled. She wore jeans and a purple and pink pullover shirt. Christmas music drifted out from another room. "Hi, Hannah. I told Mrs. Conners it was probably you." Chelsea glanced around, giggled, and said in a whisper, "You can't believe what we have to do."

"Decorate the Christmas tree."

"Four trees!" Chelsea held up four fingers for emphasis and giggled again. "Four! Who has four Christmas trees?"

Chuckling, Hannah pulled off her jacket and hung it in the closet that Chelsea showed her. She followed Chelsea down the carpeted hall lined with pictures to a huge front room with a tree that almost touched the high ceiling. A six-foot stepladder stood beside the tree. Kathy was bent over a box of ornaments, and Roxie was testing a string of tiny colored lights. They both looked up and said hello to Hannah.

"I told her," Chelsea whispered and held up four fingers.

Kathy and Roxie laughed.

"It'll be fun." Hannah touched the long soft needles on the tree. The smell of pine covered all other smells. It was as if there weren't anything left to smell but pine. She glanced around the room. "Where are the other trees?"

Roxie looked up from the string of lights that stretched across the carpet. "There are two upstairs, and the other one is outdoors in the front yard. It'll take a really tall ladder to reach the top of that one."

Just then a girl in an electric wheelchair rolled into the room. Her long brown hair was held back with a wide red ponytail band, and her forehead was wrinkled in a frown. She stopped right at the edge of the string of lights and narrowed her brown eyes. "That's an ugly tree," she snapped.

Hannah bit back a mean remark. Usually she had patience for anything, but this morning she was tired. And the tree was not ugly!

Smiling, Chelsea stepped forward. She said in her Oklahoma accent, "Hi, I'm Chelsea McCrea. That's Kathy Aber hiding in the box, Roxie Shoulders with the lights, and Hannah Shigwam over here. Who are you?"

The girl didn't answer for a long time. She lifted her chin and locked her hands in her lap. "Melinda Conners."

HILDA STAHL

Hannah darted a surprised look at Chelsea. None of them knew Mrs. Conners had a daughter.

"Do you go to Middle Lake Middle School?" Kathy asked.

"Of course not! I go to a private school. I'm in the sixth grade, but I do seventh- and eighth-grade work."

Roxie's eyes widened. "I sometimes have trouble with sixth-grade work. You must really be smart."

"I am. I read a lot." Melinda pushed the button on the arm of her chair and rolled along the edge of the lights, around them, and right up to the tree. "I find TV boring."

"We like to play games. Do you?" Hannah forced a smile. "Ever played Clue?"

Melinda frowned. "Never heard of it. I have played Scrabble with my mother. And I do have some computer games."

Chelsea rolled her eyes. "My brother Rob made up a computer game. He has about a zillion computer games, but he wanted to develop one himself."

Melinda wrinkled her nose. "How boring."

Hannah motioned to the tree and the decorations. "Want to help us?"

Her brown eyes wide, Melinda pressed back against her chair. "You've got to be kidding!"

"It's really fun!" Kathy held up a red and white

glass ball. "Look at this pretty decoration. Would you like to hang this?"

Melinda shook her head and backed her chair away. "My mother hired you girls to do it," she said in an icy voice.

"Sure. I know." Kathy held out the ball. "I thought you'd have fun helping."

"It *is* your tree," Roxie said as she started hanging the string of lights.

Hannah touched a bottom branch. "You could easily do the lower branches, and we'll do the others."

Melinda was quiet a long time. The Christmas music suddenly seemed louder. Finally she shook her head. "No . . . I'd rather just watch."

"You're welcome to help," Chelsea said, smiling.

Melinda shrugged.

"Hannah, grab that end of the lights." Roxie carefully handed the string of tiny lights to Hannah.

Hannah climbed the stepladder and draped the lights around the top of the tree and on down to the middle. Roxie took over and wound them around the bottom branches.

When Hannah finished, Chelsea climbed the ladder and set the gold and white angel on the top of the tree. She plugged it into the string of lights.

Melinda scowled. "I want the star on top!"

Roxie plugged the lights in the wall. The red,

blue, green, and yellow lights flashed on, and the angel moved back and forth as if it were looking around.

"It's beautiful!" they all said.

Melinda slapped the arm of her chair. "It's ugly! I want the star on top! I mean it!"

Chelsea shook her head. "The angel's already up there and fits just right. We'll put the star on one of the trees upstairs."

Melinda pressed her lips tightly together. "I'll tell my mother you won't do what I want."

"Your mom said she especially wanted the angel on this tree," Roxie said as she wound a string of silver beads around the tree.

"Those beads look ugly," Melinda snapped.

"They look pretty." Kathy hung a red glass ball, looked at it, and smiled.

The girls worked quietly for a while with the music in the background. Melinda kept complaining about their work. Roxie frowned at Melinda, but she kept right on complaining. Chelsea asked Melinda to help, but again she refused.

Compassion filled Hannah, and she knelt at Melinda's chair. "Why are you so angry?"

Melinda gasped. "Why do you care?"

"We all care." Hannah motioned to the Best Friends at the tree. "We care because of Jesus."

Kathy nodded. "We celebrate the birth of Jesus at Christmas. He brought peace and love and joy."

Melinda shook her head hard. "Jesus never did anything for me!"

"Yes, He did!" Roxie looked down at Melinda from the second step of the ladder. "You seem to be too angry to enjoy what He gave you."

"Well, shouldn't I be angry? Just look what He did to me!" Melinda slapped the arms of the wheelchair.

"Jesus loves you! He didn't do that to you!" Hannah caught Melinda's hand and held it firmly. "Jesus came to give life abundantly! Our enemy Satan steals, kills, and destroys. That's what the Bible says. Jesus defeated Satan, and Jesus gave us authority to stop Satan from harming us."

"Jesus worked miracles when He was here on earth," Kathy said as she hung a silver bell.

"Now he's in Heaven." Chelsea knelt down on the other side of Melinda. "The Bible says Jesus is the same yesterday, today, and forever. That means He still works miracles!"

Tears filled Melinda's eyes. "Could he . . . help me . . . walk again?"

"Nothing is impossible with God," Hannah added gently.

"Why didn't anybody tell me that?" Melinda whispered.

"Some people don't know it," Kathy said softly. "And if you don't know, you can't tell anyone."

Hannah squeezed Melinda's hand. "If you don't know, you can't receive a miracle. Read the verses in your Bible that say Jesus is your healer and your miracle-worker, then trust Him to give you a miracle. *Nothing* is impossible with God! Just have faith in Him."

"I will ask Him!" Melinda wiped away her tears with the back of her hand. "I really will!"

They talked a while longer, and then the Best Friends started to work on the tree again.

"I'll help with the bottom branches." Melinda reached into the box of ornaments and pulled out a silver bell. She rang it, sending out a clear melodious tone, then carefully hung it on a branch. "The tree really isn't ugly. I just said that because I felt so terrible."

"We know," Hannah said.

Later the girls walked upstairs while Melinda rode a lift chair on the stairs. Another wheelchair stood on the landing above, and she transferred herself from the lift to the chair.

"I have a tree in my room," Melinda said, leading the way. "I told Mom I didn't want it, but she insisted. Now I'm glad she did."

Hannah looked around Melinda's large room. The tree stood in front of a long window that looked out onto the backyard. It made the entire room smell like pine. A five-shelf bookcase full of beautifully dressed china dolls stood against a wall. An entertainment unit stood against another wall. It held a TV, VCR, CD player, cassette player, and a radio. A white telephone sat on the stand beside the bed. The room was neat and tidy, like nobody ever used it. Hannah touched the quilt rack at the foot of the bed. Her room was usually clean, but it looked lived-in all the time—especially when the twins and Lena played in their play area.

Chelsea held up the big gold star. "We'll put this at the top of your tree."

Melinda flushed. "I didn't really want the star on the tree downstairs. I was only trying to make you do what I wanted just because I wanted it."

Roxie giggled. "We know. I think everybody does that once in a while."

"I do it too often." Melinda rubbed a bough of the tree. "I get really frustrated because I can't be like other girls. I get mad at God." Melinda faced the girls and smiled. "But I'm not mad any longer now that I know He didn't make me crippled." The smile faded. "My mom is mad at God too. I'll tell her what you girls told me, and she won't me mad at Him any longer. Maybe then we can be happy again."

"How about your dad?" Roxie asked as she finished hanging the lights.

"He stays at work as much as he can so Mom can't fight with him . . . and so he can't see me." Melinda rubbed her hands up and down the sleeves of her sweater. "It makes me feel sad. It's like we aren't even a family any longer—just three people who live in the same house and never spend time together."

"You can change that," Chelsea said.

Melinda frowned questioningly. "How?"

"By praying for them." Chelsea motioned to Roxie, Kathy, and Hannah. "We always pray together when we have a problem."

Kathy reached into her pocket and pulled out a slip of paper. "It was my turn to have a Scripture for our meeting later, so I copied it down so I wouldn't forget it. Philippians 4:19—'And my God will meet all your needs according to his glorious riches in Christ Jesus.'"

"Having a happy family is a big need." Roxie held a blue glass ball and looked very serious. "I know because my family wasn't always happy. Then we accepted Jesus as our Savior, and He helped us learn to love each other and be happy." Roxie wrinkled her nose. "Sometimes I forget I'm supposed to be like Jesus."

Holding a red glass ball in her hand, Hannah turned from the tree and looked at Melinda. "We'll pray with you that your family will learn to love each other again and love God."

"Thank you." Melinda's eyes sparkled with tears. "I'd like that."

The Best Friends gathered around Melinda.

Hannah prayed, "Heavenly Father, You said if we ask anything in Jesus' name You'd give it to us. We pray that Melinda and her family will be a happy, loving family that knows Jesus as their Savior who forgives their sins. And we pray that Melinda can walk again. Thank You for answering. Help Melinda to learn Your word and trust You to do what You promised. Thank You, Heavenly Father. In Jesus' name, Amen."

Melinda brushed at her eyes. "Thank you," she whispered.

"You're welcome," the Best Friends said.

Later, after they finished the tree outdoors, both Mr. and Mrs. Conners walked into the yard to look at it. Bundled in a bright red coat, gloves, and hat, Melinda sat near the tree, smiling.

"You girls did a wonderful job." Mrs. Conners handed a check to Chelsea. "Thank you!"

Chelsea pushed the check into the pocket of her jeans. She'd cash it Monday and split it with the girls. "We're glad we could help."

"I appreciate your work," Mr. Conners said as he pushed his hands into his jacket pockets. The wind ruffled his dark hair.

Mrs. Conners rested a hand on Melinda's shoulder. "Melinda, don't be upset with me, but I asked them here so they could meet you. I see by your face they've made a difference already."

Beaming, Melinda nodded.

"Not us." Hannah shook her head. "Jesus did."

Melinda told her parents what the girls had told her. "I'm going to read the Scriptures, learn them, and believe what Jesus says."

Mr. Conners bent down and kissed Melinda's cheek. "Your mom and I will learn with you."

Her heart leaping with happiness, Hannah stepped close to the Best Friends. God answered prayer! Tomorrow she'd remind Penny Graham of that. Penny needed a miracle too.

5

Viewing the Griffin

Penny frowned into the restroom mirror at Andrews Art Academy. Her clothes were rumpled and dusty, and she knew that anyone who looked at her would know she'd slept in them the past two days. Her stomach growled with hunger, and she sucked it in until it quit. It felt like the hungry feeling touched her backbone and kept going. Maybe she should sneak to her uncle's and get clean clothes and something to eat. Fear pricked her skin, and she shook her head hard. She couldn't take a chance—not on a Sunday. Uncle Royce might catch her and lock her up; then she'd never get free. She'd have to wear what she had on and be satisfied again with a can of soda and a sandwich from the vending machine.

Tears burned her eyes as she rummaged in her bag for her hairbrush. Her teeth felt six inches thick. And she needed a shower. She glanced at her watch.

She had to get back to the lounge and hide until Hannah arrived this afternoon for the showing of the Griffin.

Just as she finished brushing her hair she heard voices outside the restroom door. Her heart zoomed to her feet, and she stood glued to the spot for a second, then leaped toward the door and pressed against the wall in back of the door. No one must see her this early! The academy wasn't open to the public until later. She'd be in major trouble if anyone found her. Nobody would believe her wild story—not that she was ready to tell anyone anyway.

The door slowly opened, and she held her breath and clasped her bag to her chest. Ice filled her veins. Two women walked in, talking about a party they'd gone to. Perfume drifted out from them. They walked directly into the stalls without looking back. Penny eased out the door into the quiet hall and stood there. Nervous perspiration dotted her face. She had to get back to the lounge to hide! Her legs seemed locked, and her feet were stuck to the floor. She forced herself to move, then ran quietly down the hall. She stopped in shock and stared at the door. It was ajar! She had closed it! She'd made sure! If someone were inside . . . Her heart sank to her feet. Where could she hide now? She listened at the door. A sound drifted out to her. Someone was definitely inside the room.

Frantically she looked around. Where could she go? She ran to the end of the hall and peeked around the corner. A huge white sign with green and black lettering stated that the Griffin was on display in the auditorium. Doors lined both sides of the corridor leading to that auditorium. She'd hide in one of those rooms! She raced past the sign and grabbed the doorknob on the first door. It wouldn't turn! Her hands felt like blocks of ice. She ran from one door to the next, frantically trying each knob. They were all locked!

A merry whistle from around the corner struck terror into her heart, and she quickly tried another door. The knob turned. She opened the door and slipped inside. It was a broom closet. The smell of dust and cleaning products choked her. She clamped her hand over her mouth and nose and waited without breathing.

What if the whistler was coming to the broom closet? She shivered and sank back weakly against a tangled mophead. "God, I know You're real, but I don't know if You hear me. If You do, help me now," she whispered urgently.

Why hadn't she listened in Sunday school so she'd know more about Jesus?

Penny bit back a moan. Her hip pressed painfully against the corner of a large sink. She moved and bumped against a broom handle. It banged against the door. She gasped, then held her breath and waited, her eyes glued to the door, her heart thudding painfully against her rib cage. The door remained closed, and slowly she relaxed.

Finally she cracked the door enough to peek out. No one was in sight. She couldn't hear whistling or voices. Cautiously she stepped into the hall. She strained her ears to hear if anyone was coming. She didn't hear anything. Taking a deep breath, she hurried toward the auditorium. Voices drifted out from the room, and the door stood open. She hoisted her bag higher onto her shoulder and cautiously peeked through the door. It was a large room with four half-circle rows of steps going down to a carpeted floor below. At the bottom of the steps the Griffin stood in the center of the carpeted area on a wooden easel. Two men were adjusting the lighting around the large framed seascape. Penny looked at the painting. The beauty of it took her breath away. If only she could paint that well!

Just then one of the men turned, and she ducked back. Trembling, she glanced around for another place to hide. She tried the door next to the auditorium. To her surprise the knob turned. She cracked open the door and peeked inside. A large desk, filing cabinet, trifold room divider, and three chairs were arranged in the small room. No one was there. Quickly she slipped inside. A door to the left of the desk leading to the auditorium stood open, and the men's voices drifted in to her.

She crept to the corner of the room where the trifold room divider stood. She eased behind it and leaned weakly against the wall. Finally she lowered her bag to the floor and rubbed her aching shoulder. Hopefully she was safe.

From the auditorium she heard one man say, "There's no way anyone could get close enough to steal the painting."

The other man said in a worried voice, "I heard there's going to be an attempt."

Penny's eyes widened in shock.

"Not on *my* shift!"

Penny shivered. If she were caught here, they might think she'd come to steal the Griffin. Maybe facing Uncle Royce would've been better than this. She shook her head. It wouldn't be! Suddenly she realized he'd probably come today, knowing she'd be here. She'd have to watch out for him—and maybe stay in hiding.

"The doors are unlocked," a woman said cheerfully inside the auditorium. "Are you ready for the public?"

"And their gum wrappers and clutter and fingers over everything," said a man with a laugh.

Penny licked her dry lips with the tip of her tongue. Soon Hannah would be here to help her. How long would she have to stay behind the screen? Somehow she'd find a way to get back out into the hall and mix in with the crowd.

Carefully, cautiously she poked her head out, then jerked back, her heart in her mouth. An old man was standing just inches from the screen with his back to her. He was tall and thin with gray hair and was dressed in a dark suit. He wasn't a guard. Did the guards know he was there?

Penny held her breath, her hand pressed to her stomach. Was the man here to steal the Griffin? Should she leap out and confront him? But she didn't dare let anyone know she was there!

She stood very still and waited.

■

About two o'clock Hannah walked into the front doors of the art academy. They'd gone to the family gathering at Parkin Hall, had dinner, talked to everyone, then left early. Ginny had wanted to leave with them, but her dad said she had to stay there. To Hannah's surprise and delight, Ginny hadn't been one bit obnoxious. They'd actually had a good time, even though Hannah had been anxious to get away.

She almost bumped into Dad pushing Burke in his stroller. Mom walked beside Dad and was keeping an eye on the twins and Lena. Several people were walking down the hall, stopping to look at the art on display on the walls.

Wide-eyed, Lena looked around. "This is a big school. I might come here someday."

Smiling, Mom patted Lena's shoulder. "It's an

art school. People who study art and design come here."

Lena slipped her hand into Hannah's. "I want to come here. I want to be like Hannah."

"Thanks." Hannah smiled at Lena, then pulled her hand away to push her hair back. "I don't see Chelsea or the others."

"They'll be here," Dad said as he wheeled the stroller out of the way of a group of people. "Glenn McCrea said he was picking up the other girls since their parents couldn't come."

"Good." Hannah smiled. "Come see my picture." Hannah led the way down the hall to the spot where her class had their work on display. She knew the Best Friends would find her. She stopped at the display and pointed to the painting of a fawn in a meadow of wild flowers.

"It's beautiful!" Lena stood on tiptoe to see better.

"I can always tell your work," Mom said proudly.

"Your ancestors would be proud of you," Dad said softly.

Hannah slipped her hand through her dad's arm and smiled at him.

They looked at the painting a long time. Finally Hannah said, "I want you to meet Mr. Jarman." She managed to keep her voice light. Could they hear her heart pound? "You'll like him."

Mom chuckled. "We've heard so much about him, it seems like we already know him."

Hannah's stomach knotted. Did they know she loved Mr. Jarman?

Just then Chelsea and Kathy rushed up, with Glenn McCrea right behind them. They looked excited and happy.

Chelsea stopped beside Hannah. "Roxie's coming later. Are we too late?"

Kathy tugged off her jacket and flopped it over her arm. "We got behind a slow driver."

"We were on our way to meet the famous Mr. Jarman," Hannah's mom said with a chuckle.

Hannah flushed.

"We want to see your painting first." Kathy glanced at the pictures on the wall. "Where is it?"

"Right there!" Lena pointed to it.

"It's beautiful!" Chelsea and Kathy said together.

Hannah glowed with pride. Having best friends like the painting was almost as important to her as having Mr. Jarman like it.

"Let's go meet the incredible Mr. Jarman." Chelsea giggled as she caught Hannah's hand and squeezed it.

Hannah self-consciously led the way to the classroom. Mr. Jarman was surrounded with people. Hannah bit back a sigh of relief. What if one of the others had teased her right then about always talking about Mr. Jarman—he might know she loved him. She headed out of the room. "He's really busy now. I'll introduce you later."

"That'll be fine," Dad said.

Kathy glanced around the room. "Is Penny Graham here?"

Hannah looked around and shook her head. "I don't see her, but when I do, I'll introduce you to her."

Looking for Penny in the crowd, Hannah led the way to the auditorium. They stopped just inside the room and stopped at the top of the steps so they could look down at the lighted painting. Hannah looked around again for Penny, but she wasn't there either. Hannah shrugged. She'd find her later. Right now she wanted to look at the Griffin and maybe see Ira Griffin himself.

Hannah studied the older men in the auditorium. Which one was Mr. Griffin? She'd seen his photograph, but she couldn't see anyone who looked like the man in the photo.

She turned her attention back to the awesome painting. She could almost hear the crash of the waves against the old ship. The lone seagull seemed so alive, she thought she heard its raucous cry. Someday her work would be as famous as Mr. Griffin's! Someday maybe she'd have her work on display at Andrews Art Academy and everyone would praise it. Maybe Penny would have one on display too.

Hannah glanced around again for Penny. Where was she? Had something terrible happened to her?

Chelsea leaned close to Hannah so she wouldn't be overheard. "We want to meet Penny. Where is she?"

Hannah shrugged. "I have no idea! Let's look for her." Hannah slipped up beside Dad. "We're going to look for my friend Penny."

"We'll meet at the front door in half an hour," Dad said as he pushed a pacifier into Burke's mouth.

Hannah glanced at her watch. "See you then." She hurried away with Chelsea and Kathy. Just outside the auditorium Hannah saw three women from her class. "Have you seen Penny Graham today?"

"No, I haven't," a gray-haired woman said.

"Maybe she's in the classroom," a Chinese woman added.

"We'll look." Hannah led the way to her classroom and peered inside. Penny wasn't there. But Mr. Jarman was. Hannah's heart jerked. She wanted to speak to him, but he was still surrounded with people. She pointed him out to Chelsea and Kathy, then reluctantly walked away.

"He's good-looking!" Chelsea nudged Hannah. "I see why you always talk about him."

Hannah's skin burned with embarrassment.

She hadn't realized she'd talked about him that much. "Let's keep looking for Penny," she said sharply.

Just then Hannah saw a tall, thin girl with honey-gold hair walking away from them. Hannah rushed to her, calling, "Penny! I've been looking for you!"

The girl turned. It wasn't Penny!

"Sorry," Hannah whispered, feeling embarrassed. "I thought you were someone else."

The girl hurried away.

Hannah sighed. "I wonder where Penny is."

"Here comes Roxie." Chelsea motioned toward the entrance.

Hannah looked, and her eyes widened. Eli, Roxie's brother, was right beside her. He had short dark hair and summer-blue eyes behind glasses and was a head taller than Roxie. He wore jeans and a green and black sweater. Hannah's whole insides quivered. Before she'd met Mr. Jarman, she'd loved Eli Shoulders. Had he come to see her work? She felt squishy all over.

Eli smiled at her. "Hi, Hannah."

"Hi." She could barely speak.

"Sorry we're so late." Roxie pulled off her jacket. "Eli took sooo long to finish dinner."

"I was hungry," he said with a laugh.

Roxie jabbed his arm. "You're always hungry."

"Come see Hannah's painting." Kathy motioned to Roxie and Eli.

"It's fantastic," Chelsea said.

Hannah flushed. Could she handle having Eli see her work? "It's nothing like the Griffin."

"But it's good," Chelsea said.

Hannah led the way to her painting. She sneaked a peek at Eli as he looked at it. She could tell he liked it. She smiled.

Just then Mr. Jarman touched Hannah's shoulder. "Hello. Are these friends of yours?"

Hannah felt weak all over. Somehow she managed to smile without fainting dead away. Today Mr. Jarman wore a dark gray suit, white shirt, and colorful tie. He made Eli look like a little boy. Hannah finally found her voice. "This is Chelsea McCrea, Kathy Aber, and Roxie and Eli Shoulders."

"Glad to meet you all. Hannah's a very special student." Mr. Jarman shook hands all the way around.

Hannah tried to think of something really intelligent to say, but no thought came to mind. It was as if her brain had shut down.

"Have you seen the Griffin?" Mr. Jarman asked the group.

"Not yet," Eli said.

"We have." Chelsea nodded. "It's really beautiful."

They talked a while longer, and finally Hannah managed to ask, "Have you seen Penny Graham?"

Mr. Jarman shook his head. "Not today."

"I've been looking for her."

"I'll tell her if I see her." Mr. Jarman smiled.

"Thanks." With her hand over her heart, Hannah watched Mr. Jarman walk away.

Eli tugged Hannah's hair. "He's too old for you, Hannah."

Flushing, she stared down at the floor. How could Eli say such a thing to her? She wanted to sink through the floor. "I have to find Penny Graham." She did too, but her thoughts sure weren't on Penny. Hannah trembled. She was thinking of Mr. Jarman. No matter how hard she tried to stop feeling the way she did about him, each time she saw him, the feelings became even stronger.

She gazed longingly toward the classroom where he'd gone. Maybe she should look for Penny there.

6

Penny in Hiding

Using a tall, broad man as a shield, Penny walked toward the auditorium. Shivers trickled up and down her spine. Several minutes earlier and about an hour after the old man had gone, she'd slipped out of hiding. She'd hunted for Hannah but couldn't find her. Maybe she was here now. Penny's stomach fluttered. What if she ran into Uncle Royce or the man who'd been following her?

Penny peeked around the tall, broad man, then ducked back. Where was Hannah? Had they missed each other in the crowd? Maybe Hannah had already looked at the Griffin and had gone home. Penny's heart sank. The man she was hiding behind stopped, and she almost bumped into him. She smelled his aftershave and felt the heat from his body. Dare she step around him and walk into the auditorium alone? She shook her head. She just couldn't!

A group of kids walked in just then. Penny bit back a gasp. The kids were from the school she attended. What if they called to her and drew attention to her? She turned away to hide her face from them.

Just then the man stepped back and bumped Penny. "Sorry." He frowned down at her, then strode away.

Penny walked cautiously into the auditorium. She glanced around at the crowd. Oh no! Aunt Peg and Uncle Royce were standing on the second step down! Penny's blood ran cold. She whirled around and ran out. When she was almost at the lounge where she'd slept, she slowed to a walk.

Clint Jarman stepped out of the lounge, a cup of coffee in his hand.

Penny jerked to a stop, startled at seeing him. "Hi," she said just above a whisper.

"Hi." He smiled. "Hannah Shigwam was looking for you."

Shigwam! That was her last name! Penny shot a look around. "Where is she?"

"I don't know. I saw her showing her painting to her friends."

Penny's heart sank. Hannah was probably too involved with her friends to help.

Mr. Jarman narrowed his eyes. "Are you all right?"

Penny nodded. What else could she do? He'd never believe her if she told him about Uncle Royce.

"Help yourself to cookies and punch in the lounge."

Her stomach cramped with hunger. "Thanks. I will."

He followed her into the lounge and refilled his cup with steaming coffee.

Penny chose the largest paper cup, filled it with red punch, and drank half of it. It was sweet, yet tangy. She ate a chocolate cookie without tasting it. The hunger pangs left, but she was still starving. She couldn't very well wolf down the entire platter of cookies right in front of Mr. Jarman.

Clint Jarman sat on a chair and motioned for Penny to sit across from him in a matching chair. "Were you in the auditorium for Ira Griffin's speech?"

Penny shook her head. "I . . . I couldn't get there." She'd heard his voice coming from the auditorium but hadn't been able to get from behind the screen to see him. She'd felt frustrated that she couldn't make out what he was saying, but was too frightened to slip from behind the screen to get close enough to hear and see him. "But I did get to see the Griffin. It's beautiful!"

Mr. Jarman nodded. "The public thinks so too."

"A lot of people came to see it."

Mr. Jarman leaned forward. "Did your family come?"

She looked sharply at him. She felt the tension in him and wondered about it. Did he know something about her? Did he know Uncle Royce's plan? "My parents are in Europe." She reached for another cookie. Her hand trembled, and she flushed. She had to get the conversation off herself. "Did your wife come?"

"She couldn't." He circled the cup with his hands. "She doesn't like art the way I do. But she does like the Griffin."

"I think everybody does." Penny drank two more glasses of punch and ate four more cookies while Clint Jarman talked about painting and himself. Her mind drifted to Uncle Royce and his plans for her. The cookie in her mouth turned to dust. She washed it down and couldn't take another bite.

Mr. Jarman reached out to her. "Are you sure you're all right?"

She nodded. For some reason she didn't trust him.

"I could drive you home if you're not well."

"I'm fine . . . Really . . . I think I'd better go. I could use some fresh air."

Mr. Jarman stood. "I could let you out a back door if you want."

"That would be great!" Penny smiled. Uncle Royce wouldn't see her if she sneaked out the back

71

door. She grabbed her bag and followed Mr. Jarman to the nearest exit. She looked around but didn't see anyone she knew.

"You seem nervous, Penny." Mr. Jarman unlocked the door and held it open. Cold air rushed in. Frowning, he blocked her way. "Are you in trouble?"

She shook her head. She wasn't about to tell him anything.

Finally he moved and let her pass. "See you tomorrow afternoon."

She nodded as she tugged her jacket out of her bag and slipped it on. She heard the door lock behind her, and she breathed a sigh of relief. A paper blew into the corner at the back of the building. A car honked, and she shot a look toward the street. Maybe Hannah would be in the parking lot.

Penny dashed around the huge brick building, her bag slapping against her side. Anxiously she looked around the parking lot, but Hannah wasn't there. Penny stood beside a red Ford and forced back tears of frustration. She looked toward the front doors. Hannah stood just inside! Penny ran to the door and quickly slipped inside.

Hannah turned and called in relief, "Penny!"

She caught Hannah's arm. "Help me!"

"I will . . . What's wrong . . . What can I do?"

Penny looked over Hannah's shoulder and saw Uncle Royce and Aunt Peg walking toward them.

They were in deep conversation and didn't notice her. But if they looked up, they'd see her for sure. With a strangled cry she shoved open the heavy glass door and ran outdoors, her hair streaming behind her, her eyes wide with fear. She ducked behind the first car, bent over, and ran back around the building. She sagged against the back of the building, her chest heaving and her face red from exertion. A sound near the back door got her attention. A tall, thin man was coming out the door—the same man she'd seen earlier while hiding behind the screen. Her eyes widened and she wanted to run, but her legs refused to move.

He walked toward her, his head down, his shoulders bent. He would certainly see her! She gasped but still couldn't move.

He looked up in alarm. His brows rose. "Are you spying on me?" he asked gruffly.

She swallowed hard. "No!"

Slowly he relaxed, then shrugged. "What are you doing back here all alone?"

She searched her mind for an answer. Finally she said, "Waiting for a friend."

His dark eyes narrowed, and he stepped toward her. "Do I know you?"

She sidled away from him. "I don't know you, and you don't know me."

"You look very familiar to me."

Her mouth dry, she shook her head.

"What's your name?" His voice was sharp and demanding.

Fear pricked her skin. Maybe the man was working with the man who was following her. Or maybe he was working for Uncle Royce! She bit back a terrified scream, turned, and ran back around the school.

"Wait! Wait! I didn't mean to frighten you!"

Penny ducked down behind a car until she was sure the man was gone, then walked cautiously across the parking lot, keeping out of sight behind the cars. Suddenly she realized it would be the perfect time to go to Uncle Royce's house and get Daddy's itinerary, her money, and her clean clothes. If she hurried, she'd be in and out before her uncle and aunt got back home.

Penny ran the two blocks, glancing over her shoulder every few minutes to see if her uncle was coming. The only car she spotted was a blue Chevy. She tried to relax, but every nerve was tight and felt ready to snap.

At the house she glanced around to make sure no one saw her who could tell Uncle Royce she'd been there. Trembling, she unlocked the front door and slipped inside. The smell of coffee filled the room. Her heart beat so loud, she was sure they could hear it back at the academy. The clock bonged, and she jumped. The floor creaked, and her heart almost leaped through her jacket. She ran to her room and grabbed clothes from her dresser and closet and stuffed them into her roll bag. She dropped in her toothbrush, toothpaste, shampoo and conditioner, and other things she knew she'd need. She looked longingly at the shower but didn't dare take time for one.

Trembling, she ran to the den for her money and the itinerary. Where would Uncle Royce hide them? Frantically she searched through the papers on the cluttered desk and in the drawers, but couldn't find what she was looking for.

A car door slammed, and her heart plunged to her feet. She peeked out the window. Uncle Royce and Aunt Peg were home!

Penny jerked back from the window. Fear pricked her skin, and chills ran over her body. Did they suspect she was in the house? She stood rooted to the spot. Her mind whirled with ideas on what to do to get away. She knew they'd come in the back door through the garage, so that would give her a chance to slip out the front door. If only she'd found the money and the itinerary! She'd have to leave without them.

She grabbed her pack and her roll bag and ran to the front door. She silently slipped out. Cold air blew against her, and she shivered. She ran down the steps onto the sidewalk and dashed away. Had they seen her leave? Would they follow her in their car? She looked over her shoulder every few seconds.

There was only a boy on a bike and a white car in sight.

A few minutes later she dashed through the front door of the academy and hurried to the lounge. Thankfully it was empty. She quickly pushed her things behind the sofa and crept after them. She stretched out, her heart drumming painfully. Before she could catch her breath, she heard someone walk into the lounge. Had someone spotted her? She held her hand over her mouth and strained her ears to hear every sound.

"I'm sure I saw the Graham girl walk in here," said a man.

Penny's eyes widened. Someone had seen her! Someone was looking for her!

"She's not here," said another man, sounding disappointed.

Penny shivered. Who were the men? What did they want with her?

"I was sure I saw her."

Penny felt a scream rising inside her.

"I might as well walk through the school again. If I don't spot her, I'll give up and pick her up Monday in school."

Penny's nerves tightened even more. Pick her up Monday? What did the man want with her?

"I hope you're wrong about her."

Penny lay stone-still. Wrong about her? Wrong about what? She heard the men walk out of the room, and then all was quiet except the thump of her heart and the distant sound of voices. Who were the men and what did they want with her?

7

Ira Griffin

Frowning, Hannah stepped outside the academy. Cold wind made her shiver. Where was Penny? A car honked.

"Penny!" Hannah walked away from the building toward the parking area. "Penny, do you hear me?" Hannah waited, but Penny didn't answer and didn't come to her. "I wonder where she is."

Slowly Hannah walked back inside. Who or what had frightened Penny away? Deep in thought, Hannah tucked her hair behind her ears as she walked slowly down the hall. She ran right into someone. She looked up and gasped. "Eli! I wasn't watching where I was going."

He chuckled as he pushed his glasses up on his nose. "I could tell."

"Sorry." She wanted to sink out of sight.

He peered at her questioningly. "What's wrong?"

"Did I say something was wrong?" Hannah asked, taking a step back.

"You look upset. And you're not with your shadows."

Hannah giggled. He meant Kathy, Roxie, and Chelsea. Eli liked teasing them about always being together. "We're best friends, not shadows."

"So you say." Eli grinned. "I don't think I ever saw four girls stick so close together."

"They went to the restroom."

Eli glanced at his watch. "How much longer before we go home?"

"I don't know. Are you bored?"

"Maybe a little." Grinning, he held out his hand. "Not that I don't like your work. It's just that I can't wait to drive again. It's great having a license."

"I'll be glad when I'm sixteen. Was it hard to pass the test?"

Eli shook his head. "I only got one question wrong on my written test. And that was because it was worded funny. I couldn't tell what they really meant."

Hannah smiled. "When will you get a car of your own?"

Eli chuckled. "I asked Dad this morning. He says we'll look for one soon. I'll help pay for it with my afterschool and summer jobs." He tapped

Hannah on the shoulder. "I might even give you a ride."

"Thanks."

Just then Clint Jarman stuck his head out of the classroom door and called, "Hannah, could you come here please?"

Hannah's eyes lit up.

"What does he want?" Eli said in a low, tight voice.

Hannah hurried away without saying a word to Eli. She stopped just inside the classroom and smiled at Mr. Jarman. All her plans to stop loving him flew right out of her head.

Mr. Jarman smiled. "I'm sorry to take you away from your friend, but I need your help."

"You do?" Her pulse leaped. He was actually asking her for help!

Mr. Jarman cleared his throat. "I can't get away right now, but I promised to deliver this to someone who's waiting for me outside the back door." He held up a long white business envelope. "Would you do it for me?"

"Of course!" She'd do almost anything for him.

Mr. Jarman stepped closer to her and lowered his voice. "This is a secret mission."

Her eyes flashed with excitement. A secret mission for Clint Jarman! What more could she ask for?

"It's for Ira Griffin."

Hannah gasped and almost fell over. "Ira Griffin?" she whispered in awe.

Clint nodded.

Hannah trembled. She was going to deliver something to the great Ira Griffin! Clint Jarman trusted her enough to ask her to take Ira Griffin a message!

Clint frowned slightly and looked quickly around, then back at Hannah. "It's very confidential."

"Really?" Her feet felt mere inches off the floor.

"Don't let anyone know he's still here."

"I won't! I mean it . . . I won't," she whispered.

"I let him out the back door, then remembered I had this for him. I asked him to wait for me." Clint handed the envelope to Hannah. "Give this to him—tell him I asked you to deliver it to him."

With chills of delight running over her, Hannah took the envelope. One end felt heavy, as if a coin were taped to a paper inside. Wouldn't the Best Friends love this! She couldn't wait to tell them. Then she remembered it was confidential. She couldn't tell them. This was a secret between her, Mr. Jarman, and Ira Griffin! Was she dreaming?

"Here's the key to the back exit." Clint handed it to her. "Then come to the auditorium, tell me you gave the envelope to him, and return the key to me."

"I will."

He patted her shoulder and smiled. "Thank you."

For a minute she couldn't move. She felt his hand on her shoulder even after he took it off. Tingling all over, she walked out of the room as if she were walking on air. She was doing a favor for Clint Jarman! And she was going to see Ira Griffin up close!

"Hannah!"

She turned to find Eli Shoulders walking toward her. She frowned at the interruption.

"Where are you going?" Eli asked.

"Just outdoors. I won't be long."

"Want me to go with you?"

Panic rushed through her. He couldn't go with her, but she didn't want to make him feel bad by saying so. "That's all right. I'll meet you later in the auditorium."

Eli peered closely at her. "What's going on, Hannah?"

"What do you mean?" Oh, but she sounded sooo innocent!

"You look . . . strange."

"I'm all right . . . Really." But was she?

Eli shrugged and walked back the way he'd come.

Sighing in relief, Hannah rushed toward the back exit, unlocked the door, and slipped out. She shivered in the cold air. Why hadn't she grabbed her jacket? She glanced around at the bushes and the sidewalk. Nobody was in sight. Where was Ira Griffin? Would she know him if she saw him? She'd missed his speech at the auditorium because she's been looking for Penny. "Mr. Griffin?" Her voice came out in a hoarse whisper. She cleared her throat. "Mr. Griffin?"

"Here."

Gasping, she whirled around just as he stepped from behind the bushes. He was tall and thin, wore glasses, and was dressed in a gray suit.

He frowned suspiciously at her. "What do you want? How'd you know where to find me?"

Hesitantly she held the envelope out to him. "Clint Jarman asked me to give you this. He couldn't come himself, but he said you'd have a message for him."

"It took him long enough." Mr. Griffin grabbed the envelope and ripped it open. A key fell to the sidewalk.

Hannah quickly picked it up and held it out to Ira Griffin. Was she dreaming? Was the great man really standing right there in front of her?

Ira Griffin clutched the key. "Tell him I'll take him up on his offer for a place to stay—and that I won't be able to come back Monday to talk to his classes."

"You won't?" Hannah's heart plunged to her

feet. "I'm one of the students. I would love to hear you talk about art!"

"Nonsense! Why would you want to listen to an old man spout on and on about nothing?"

"About nothing!" Her eyes wide, Hannah tucked her shiny black hair behind her ears. "I love your work! I'd like to paint as well as you." She looked him squarely in the eye. "And with God's help, I will!"

Sudden tears sparkled in Mr. Griffin's brown eyes behind his dark framed glasses. "I remember saying those very same words years ago to an artist I admired." He scowled at her. "You look too young to be so serious."

Hannah squared her shoulders. "I'm young, but I am very serious. So is another girl my age who is in the same class."

His face hardened. "I don't have the time or the inclination to stand here and listen to you go on and on about this." He pushed past her, strode to the end of the building, and turned toward the teachers' parking area.

Hannah hesitated, then dashed after Mr. Griffin. Maybe she could say something to convince him to come to their class. She ran around the corner of the building, then stopped short when she saw Mr. Griffin and a dark-haired woman in her forties in a heated argument. Hannah ducked out of sight behind a dumpster.

"Get away from me, Cara North!" Ira Griffin shouted. "I told Rob I'm breaking my contract with him. We have nothing more to do with each other."

Hannah gasped as she peeked around the dumpster. What was going on? Should she run to Mr. Griffin's aid?

Cara North shook her finger at Ira Griffin. "You're making a big mistake, Ira! You can't quit painting. We both know that. It's a waste of talent!"

"Talent!" He spat out the word. "You don't care about my talent! You like the money it brings. You and Rob get your share, and you don't want to lose it. Now, let me get in the car and go."

She grabbed his arm. "You can't just disappear!"

He shook her off. "Watch me." He tried to push his car key into the door lock, but she grabbed his arm, and the key fell to the pavement. His face turned brick-red. "Get away or I'll call the security guard!"

Hannah bit her lip. Should she help Mr. Griffin? Would he be angry if she tried?

Cara North clamped her hand tightly over her purse. "You'll be sorry for this, Ira. I'll use force if I must to get you back at your easel."

He picked up the key and unlocked the car door.

"I mean it, Ira. I know something about your

past that you think no one knows. I know, and with that I can force you to do what I want."

Hannah bit back a cry of alarm.

His face ashen, Ira Griffin faced Cara squarely. "What do you know about my past?"

Hannah wrapped her arms around herself to hold back shivers of cold and fear. What could the woman mean?

"There's nothing to know," Ira Griffin snapped.

Cara smiled wickedly. "Isn't there?"

"You're bluffing!"

"Am I?" Cara pushed her hands deep into her coat pockets. "I know about your daughter."

"I have no daughter!" Ira's voice boomed out, his face dark with rage.

Hannah gasped. In all she'd read about Ira Griffin she'd never read he had a daughter.

Cara shook her finger at Ira. "Yes, you do! And she has a daughter . . . Your only granddaughter." Cara lifted her chin.

Ira helplessly shook his head.

"I'll give you this weekend to make up your mind, and then I'll hold your granddaughter prisoner until you do as I say."

Hannah trembled. Was the woman serious? She certainly looked and sounded serious.

Ira gripped Cara's arms. "Lies don't scare me. I have no family."

"I can prove you do. I've seen your grand-daughter. She has talent in art just like you."

"Stop!"

Cara pulled away from Ira Griffin. "You have this weekend to decide." She walked away from him, then turned back. "I have a man working with me who hates your granddaughter enough to do anything I ask." Cara turned back and strode away.

Hannah's head spun. What should she do?

Just then Ira Griffin groaned and sank against the car, his hand on his heart.

With a cry Hannah dashed to him and caught his arm. His face was gray and pinched. "Are you all right?"

"I don't know," he said weakly. "I have to sit down."

She opened his car door and helped him onto the seat. "I didn't plan to eavesdrop, but I heard the argument you had with that woman. Is there anything I can do to help you?"

"No."

"Shall I get Mr. Jarman?"

Ira Griffin shook his head. "I must get away from here so I can think. I have to call my daughter and learn the truth."

Hannah forced back a gasp. He did have a daughter! "I wish I could help you more."

Ira Griffin smiled. "Thank you."

"I'll be praying for you."

"You do that." He started the car and drove away.

Shivering with cold, Hannah ran to the back door and let herself in. The warmth wrapped around her. She looked at the key in her hand. She'd give it and the message to Mr. Jarman. Should she tell him about the argument? She shook her head. If Mr. Griffin wanted Mr. Jarman to know, he'd tell him.

Just as Hannah walked past the lounge, Penny Graham stuck her head out and called, "Hannah, come here!"

Relieved, Hannah hurried over to her. "I've been looking all over for you!"

Penny caught Hannah's arm. "Could I please *please* go home with you? I'll explain later."

Hannah hesitated only a second, then nodded. She knew her family would want to help Penny just like they helped anyone else in need. "I have to go to the auditorium first. Come with me."

"I don't dare! Somebody might see me."

Hannah frowned. "Is that man still following you?"

"He might be."

"Then wait here. I'll be back in a few minutes to get you."

Penny bit her lip. "Please don't tell anyone you saw me!"

"I won't." Hannah hurried away. Was Penny

really in danger, or was it her imagination? Hannah brushed aside thoughts of Penny for the time being, then found Mr. Jarman. She gave him the key and quickly told him what Mr. Griffin had said.

"Thanks, Hannah. I owe you one." Mr. Jarman squeezed her shoulder and smiled.

Her legs turned to water, and she thought she'd fall at his feet. Then she thought about Penny, and strength rushed through her again. "I'll see you tomorrow in class."

He smiled and nodded, then turned to someone trying to get his attention.

Hannah walked out of the auditorium and right into the Best Friends. "Come with me," she said in a hushed voice. "I have to get Penny."

"So you finally found her," Roxie said.

"Did you really find a mystery?" Chelsea asked with a giggle.

Hannah nodded. "And I'm afraid this one means danger for someone."

Danger? Had she really used that word? She shivered.

8

Locked In

Penny's bag almost dropped from her lifeless fingers to the Andrews Art Academy lobby floor, but she clung to it and stared in horror at Aunt Peg standing only a few feet away. She was looking at a painting on the wall. Uncle Royce wasn't in sight. Penny fled toward the heavy glass front door. She must not let Aunt Peg see her! But maybe Aunt Peg had spotted her already! Could Uncle Royce be lurking nearby to grab her? When had they returned to the academy? She'd left them at home not more than an hour ago.

Suddenly a strong hand gripped Penny's arm and almost pulled her off her feet. Shrieking, she turned her head and stared in terror at Uncle Royce. He was a head taller than she was, and he wore a dark suit that fit snugly across his broad shoulders. A striped tie hung loosely around his thick neck.

"Don't make another sound," he growled close to her ear.

"Let me go," she whispered hoarsely. She looked wildly around for help. Where was Hannah? People were walking to their cars, but no one noticed her, and no one came to help her.

"You're going home with us. I can't let you stay with a friend again. What would your father say?"

She stopped struggling. Uncle Royce had no idea she'd overheard him earlier today. Maybe she could go with him, then run away again later. She lifted her face to him and tried to look very innocent. "I have to tell my friend I can't stay with her."

"Where is this friend?"

"I told her I'd meet her in the lounge."

"When you don't show up, she'll know you can't stay with her." Royce pushed Penny out the door. Cold air struck her, and she shivered.

"I could wait right here for her!"

Royce laughed gruffly. "Do you take me for an idiot? I'm not letting you out of my sight." He walked her to his car, opened the passenger door, and pushed Penny into the backseat. The wind ruffled his thin gray hair. "Sit still and don't make a scene." He slammed the door.

She cringed against the seat, her green eyes wide in fear. Uncle Royce no longer pretended to be friendly or kind. It was as if he didn't care if she knew he was going to do something terrible to her.

She shivered and locked her fingers together in her lap. Silently she prayed for help. Maybe Hannah would try to find her. Or would Hannah shrug it off and forget all about her?

Royce slipped into the car on the driver's side. "Keep your mouth shut back there or you'll be sorry."

Peg climbed in on the passenger side, a frown on her round face. "I'm sick and tired of chasing after you, Penny. I feed you and keep your clothes clean, and look at the thanks I get!" Peg scowled, then settled in place. "Let's get home. I want to watch that mystery movie on TV tonight."

"No show on TV is as exciting as real life." Chuckling, Royce drove out of the parking lot.

With a sick feeling in the pit of her stomach, Penny stared straight ahead. The heater hummed, blasting heat throughout the car. Her head spun as she tried to decide what to do and how to act. She had to keep Uncle Royce from knowing how upset and frightened she really was. She cleared her throat and forced herself to speak. "Did you see the painting on display in the auditorium?" The words almost choked her.

Royce shot a frown back at her, then turned to watch his driving. "I saw it." He laughed dryly. "I even know who painted it."

Penny frowned. Of course he knew. Everybody

knew it was a Griffin. Did Uncle Royce mean he knew Mr. Griffin personally?

Peg shook her gray head. "To think that painting is worth all that money! I'd rather have a painting of a garden full of flowers. I like flowers better than water. I just can't believe a painting like that could be worth that much money."

Penny bit back a sharp retort. They didn't know anything about art, and nothing she'd say would make a difference. They thought she was wasting her time going to the academy to learn more about art.

Royce pulled into the garage, got out of the car, and opened the back door for Penny. He gripped her arm and pushed her into the warm kitchen that smelled like coffee.

Penny pulled away from Royce like he was a rattlesnake. "Let me go!"

"Don't think you're so high and mighty." Royce tugged a strand of her blonde hair. "My brother sure raised you wrong—letting you get so mouthy and all."

Penny bit her tongue to keep from saying anything that would anger Uncle Royce even more. Why had Daddy put her in his charge? She should've stayed with friends in Boston.

"We'll have supper in a few minutes." Peg hung her coat in the closet and set her purse on the shelf. She shook her finger at Penny. "I don't know if I can eat after the scare you gave us—disappearing and all."

Penny ducked her head to hide the anger in her eyes. "I'm sorry, Aunt Peg." Penny sounded contrite and humble—far from what she was really feeling.

"As you should be!" Peg tied a flowered apron around her ample waist. She opened the refrigerator and looked inside. "We're having leftovers, and I don't want to hear any complaints."

"You won't hear any from me." Royce turned to Penny. "You won't have a chance to leave again. Get that through your head."

Penny shivered.

Royce poured himself a cup of coffee, sat at the small kitchen table, and sipped it slowly. He opened a bag of chocolate cookies on the table and took out a handful. He dipped one in his coffee and sucked it noisily.

Penny moved restlessly from one foot to the other. She wanted to go to her room, but she was afraid they'd stop her. She forced a smile at Peg. "Would you like help with supper?"

Penny frowned. "You haven't been a bit of help so far. Why break a good record?" She spooned cold mashed potatoes into the hot butter in the skillet. She added leftover chicken bits and buttered corn.

Penny edged toward the door. "I'd better wash for supper."

Royce jumped up. "I'll go with you."

"That's not necessary," Penny said stiffly.

Royce pushed the rest of a cookie into his mouth and swallowed. He rubbed a large hand over his face. "I'd hate for you to run out on us again."

Penny lifted her head and walked out of the kitchen, into the living room, and toward her room. How could she endure this a minute longer? She stopped at her bedroom door. "I want to change my clothes."

"Fine. Go right ahead."

She frowned, walked into her room, and closed the door in Royce's face. She slowly walked across the room. She heard a click and spun around, expecting Royce to be there. But the door remained closed. She heaved a sigh of relief.

Slowly she walked to her bed. The room was nothing like hers at home, but at least she did have privacy and a bathroom of her own. The bed was still unmade from when she'd left Friday morning. She lifted the white spread off the carpet and dropped it in a heap at the foot of her bed. Two sweaters lay on her chair with a pair of jeans draped across the back. One bedroom slipper lay near the open closet door, and the other peeked out from under the bed. With a sigh she sank to the edge of the bed. How could she call Hannah to beg for help? She had no phone in her room.

"Hannah," Penny whispered. What was her last name? Penny frowned in thought and suddenly remembered it. "Shigwam. Shigwam." She didn't want to forget again. Maybe later she'd have a chance to use the phone in the kitchen.

The room grew dark, and she clicked on the bedside lamp. She pulled off her clothes and changed into clean ones. She brushed her hair and pulled it back and held it in place with a wide pony-tail band. Her stomach growled. She'd have to eat. Already she'd gone without food too long.

Sighing unhappily, she walked to the door. How she hated to face Royce and Peg! Penny's stom-ach growled again. Reluctantly she reached for the doorknob. Her hand trembled. She started to turn the knob, but it wouldn't turn. She tried again, then gasped as she realized she was locked in! Her hand at her throat, she fell back. "It's locked," she whis-pered weakly. "Now what'll I do?"

With a groan she wrapped her arms around herself and rocked back and forth, back and forth. Silently she prayed for help.

At long last she knuckled away her tears and rapped loudly on the door. She waited, then knocked louder. "Open this door! I'm locked in! Get me out right now!"

She waited, barely breathing. Finally a key grated in the lock, and slowly Peg opened the door. She walked in carrying a tray of food.

"Don't think you can order me around, Penny

Graham! Sit down and eat so I can get back to watching TV."

Penny dropped to the chair at her desk, picked up a fork, and took a big bite of warmed-over mashed potatoes, chicken, and corn. It tasted delicious. With her mouth full she said, "Why's my door locked?"

"So you can't leave again without permission."

Penny swallowed her food and scowled at Peg. "Daddy will be angry when I tell him about this."

Chuckling, Royce stuck his head in the door. "Wait until you hear what *they* did to you!"

"Royce!" Peg grabbed his arm. "Don't say anything you'll regret later!"

He shook free. "I won't be sorry. *They* will!"

Penny shook her head to stop the confused buzz of thoughts. What was Royce talking about?

Peg caught Royce's arm again. "Let's get back to the TV."

The food forgotten on her plate, Penny frowned at Royce. "I thought you and Daddy made up your fight."

"He thinks so too." Chuckling, Royce jangled the change in his pockets. "That's the beauty of it. Jason Graham, the great Senator of Massachusetts, is out on a famous mission for peace, and he doesn't even know there's no peace in his own household." Royce laughed and shook his head.

Penny trembled. "What are you talking about?"

Peg shook Royce's arm. "Leave her alone!"

Penny turned helplessly to Peg. "Please don't let him hurt me."

"I'm not going to hurt you," Royce snapped. "You're locked in so you can't disappear again."

"You don't have to lock me in. I'll stay right here."

Royce snorted. "I'll believe that the day Michigan turns into a desert." He started to walk away, then turned back. "Secrets can be used for sweet revenge, dear niece."

Penny's blood turned to ice. "What secrets?"

Royce shrugged and walked away.

Peg shook her head, closed the door, and locked it.

Penny sank back against the chair. "What secrets?" she whispered weakly.

■

Hannah rushed to Roxie and Eli waiting at the door of the academy. Dad had agreed to let her ride home with Eli, so Hannah's family had left when Burke started being fussy. Now Hannah looked helplessly at Eli and Roxie. "Penny's gone! And she said she'd wait for me!"

"That's really weird." Roxie slipped on her jacket. "Maybe she didn't need help after all."

"But she was sooo scared!"

"Or pretended to be," Eli said, rattling the car keys. "We have to go, girls. It's getting late."

Roxie jabbed his arm. "It's not that late! You're anxious to drive again, we know."

Eli shrugged. "Well . . ."

Hannah managed to laugh. She knew Eli was excited about driving, but right now her mind was full of Penny Graham. "I don't know what to do about Penny."

"Tell the police about her," Eli said.

"No." Hannah shook her head. "She doesn't want that."

"You might find this exciting, but I'm getting bored." Roxie pushed open the heavy glass door. "Let's go!"

Hannah bit her lip and finally nodded. It wasn't right to keep Eli and Roxie waiting.

Eli didn't move. "We could drive to her house and check on her."

"Great idea!" Hannah laughed in relief.

"Do you know her address?" Roxie asked, stepping away from the door to let two women out.

"No. I've been to her house though. I could get the address from Mr. Jarman!" Hannah glanced down the hall. "I'll go ask right now!"

"Don't take all night," Roxie said impatiently.

"Don't forget we're here waiting," Eli added.

Flushing at their implication, Hannah ran to

the classroom and slipped inside. Clint Jarman stood at the window, his hands in his pockets.

He turned with a frown, then smiled. "Hannah! I thought you'd gone."

As usual, her knees turned to soft marshmallows. "I was ready to, but I need to see Penny Graham. Can I get her address and phone number from you?"

"Sure." Mr. Jarman pulled a book from his desk drawer and flipped it open. He quickly jotted down the information and handed it to Hannah.

"Thanks." Hannah couldn't move for a minute. With a self-conscious laugh she turned away and hurried back to Roxie and Eli. "I'll try to get her on the phone first."

"I'll go warm the car. Roxie, you wait for Hannah." Eli pushed open the door, letting in a blast of cold air. "Don't be too long."

Roxie shrugged and impatiently followed Hannah to the lounge.

Hannah was thankful the lounge was empty. She punched the phone number and held her breath until someone answered it. A man barked into the phone, and she jumped. "May I speak to Penny Graham, please?"

"She's not here." The man's voice was gruff and impatient.

"This is Hannah Shigwam. Penny and I attend art classes together. It's important that I speak to her.

I'll leave my number so she can call me when she gets in."

"Don't bother."

"It's no bother." Hannah hesitated. Should she tell the man she was afraid Penny was in real danger? Maybe he'd help her. Before Hannah could speak, she heard the man hang up. Frowning thoughtfully, she slowly replaced the receiver. Sighing, she pushed the paper into her pocket and told Roxie what he'd said. "He sounds mean."

"We could drive to her house like Eli said."

Hannah's eyes lit up. "Yes! Let's do!" If she talked to Penny's uncle in person and asked him to help Penny, surely he'd want to.

Hannah and Roxie ran to the car, shivering in the cold. Hannah sat in the backseat and Roxie the front. The car was already warm. They quickly told Eli their plan.

"It's only two blocks from here," Hannah said.

"Let's do it! I don't mind a bit." Eli grinned back at Hannah, then drove out of the parking lot and followed the directions Hannah gave him to get to Penny's house.

Hannah peered out at the lights shining from the windows of the houses they passed. Soon Eli stopped at the curb outside Penny's house and looked back at Hannah. "Now what?"

"I guess go see if she's there." Hannah's mouth

felt cottonball dry. "I hope nothing's happened to her."

"If it were Halloween we could say 'Trick or Treat' for our reason for being here." Roxie giggled.

Eli frowned at Roxie. She stopped giggling and shrugged. Eli looked thoughtfully at the house. "We'll just say we came to talk to Penny."

"Sure. What's the big deal?" Hannah opened the car door before she lost her courage. Somewhere down the street a dog barked. The smell of wood smoke from a nearby house drifted through the air.

"Chelsea and Kathy will be mad they missed this." Roxie grinned as she fell into step with Hannah.

Eli shook his head. "Do you girls have this kind of adventure often?"

"No," Roxie said.

"Sometimes," Hannah said.

They both laughed, then stopped suddenly as they reached the door.

Eli knocked, and they all three waited nervously.

The door burst open, and Royce Graham blocked the light from inside. The TV blared behind him. "What do you want?" he snapped.

Hannah swallowed hard. "We came to see Penny."

"She's not here!" Royce started to close the door, but Eli grabbed it.

"When will she be back?" Eli asked.

"I don't know." Royce glared at them, then slammed the door.

Hannah shivered. "He's mean. But I still think we should tell him Penny's in danger."

Trembling, Roxie tugged Hannah's arm. "Let's get out of here!"

"I'd hate to have him for an uncle," Eli said as they walked to the car. "He might not even care if Penny's in trouble."

Hannah hesitated as she looked back at the house. "She said she was being followed. What if the man following her kidnapped her?"

"Should we call the police even if she doesn't want us to?" Roxie asked.

Hannah shook her head. "I guess not. We'd better just go home. The police wouldn't like it if we sent them on a wild goose chase."

"We can pray for her," Eli said.

Roxie smiled. She liked hearing her brother say that.

Hannah nodded. Silently she prayed for Penny as Eli drove them home.

Maybe Penny would be at the academy tomorrow and say everything was just fine. But somehow Hannah didn't think so.

Hannah leaned her head back against the seat and prayed again for Penny.

9

A Surprise Visit

Hannah walked to the kitchen where she knew Mom was putting dry great northern beans to soak so she could make baked beans tomorrow. The whole family loved Mom's homemade baked beans.

At the counter Mom rubbed lotion on her hands and smiled. "What's wrong, Hannah? You look upset."

Hannah sighed heavily. "I've had a strange day."

"Tell me about it." Mom poured two glasses of orange juice and sat down at the table. She kept a glass for herself and set the other one across from her for Hannah. "Sit down and relax."

Taking a deep breath, Hannah sat down. She smelled the orange juice and Mom's lotion. "I don't know where to start."

"What's bothering you the most?"

"Penny Graham . . . I'm really worried about

her." Hannah told Mom about Penny. When she finished, she drank half a glass of orange juice, then dabbed her mouth with a white paper napkin from the wooden holder in the center of the table. "I wish I knew what to do."

"It does sound like Penny's in trouble, but it would probably be better to leave it up to her uncle. He might sound gruff and mean, but he might not be at all. Some people just seem like that."

"I guess."

"It's very thoughtful of you to want to help Penny, but maybe you can't do anything for her."

"I'm going to try, Mom." Hannah finished her orange juice. She still didn't know what to do for Penny. Maybe Mom was right; maybe there wasn't anything she could do.

"What else happened today?" Mom asked.

Hannah told Mom about seeing Mr. Griffin. "Mom, he really is thinking of quitting painting. Isn't that terrible?"

"Yes. Did he say why?"

"He doesn't think he has anything else to offer." Hannah moaned. "How can he say that? His work is awesome!"

"He probably has his reasons."

"None of them could be good enough!" Hannah remembered Cara North who'd threatened Mr. Griffin, but she didn't tell Mom about that. Mr. Griffin didn't want it told.

Mom cleared her throat. "Hannah, I must speak to you about something very important." Mom fingered her empty glass. "But it's a little embarrassing to you."

Hannah stiffened. "What is it?"

Mom locked her hands on the table in front of her. "I know you think a lot of your art instructor, Mr. Jarman."

"He's a nice man."

"I'm sure he is." Mom leaned forward. "Hannah, don't let your feelings get away from you. He's married, and he's much older than you."

"I know," Hannah whispered.

"Don't fantasize about loving him and marrying him."

Hannah wanted to run and hide, but she sat still, her hands locked in her lap.

"Doing wrong starts in your thoughts first." Mom looked very serious. "You first think about how wonderful Mr. Jarman is. Then you think about wanting to be with him more. Soon you think about being married to him."

Hannah flushed painfully. How did Mom know?

Mom gently touched Hannah's hand. "Learn to control your thoughts and you'll be able to control your feelings and actions."

Hannah ducked her head. "I don't try to think about him like that—it just happens."

"I understand. I honestly do. That's why I'm talking to you." Mom brushed away a tear that clung to her dark lashes. "But you're not alone. Jesus is always with you. Always! Ask Him to help you control your thoughts. You know He wants to help you in every area of your life—even your thought life."

"I guess I didn't think about that," Hannah whispered. But did she honestly want to stop loving Mr. Jarman? The thought startled her. Did she like loving Mr. Jarman because it made her feel good?

"You'll do the right thing, Hannah." Mom smiled. "You always do."

Hannah thought about the time she'd broken the special pickle dish and had let the twins take the blame. It had been the first time she'd ever done such a thing, and she'd promised herself it would be the last. She'd felt terrible until she finally found the courage to tell her parents the truth. But this was different. She didn't feel terrible for loving Mr. Jarman. Maybe it was all right to *love* him—just not to be *in love* with him and dream about marrying him. Yes! That was the right answer. Silently she asked Jesus to help her control her thoughts so she wouldn't daydream about marrying Mr. Jarman.

Hannah smiled. "Thanks for talking to me, Mom."

"You're very welcome." Mom walked around the table and kissed Hannah on the head. "I love you. That's why I warned you. It was hard for me to bring it up because I knew it would embarrass you. But I had to because I do love you. I want you to learn early to control your thought life so you don't have trouble with it later."

Just then the doorbell rang. Hannah jumped up. "It's probably Chelsea and Roxie."

"You girls can have the kitchen." Mom kissed Hannah again. "Have fun."

"Thanks. We will." Hannah hurried to open the door. Chelsea and Roxie rushed in, shivering. Kathy usually went to church on Sunday nights, so she couldn't come.

"It's cold out there!" Chelsea hung her jacket in the hall closet, then stepped aside so Roxie could do the same.

"Come in the kitchen. It's the only room where we can have privacy." Hannah led the way. Sometimes it was very hard to have such a large family. She and the girls couldn't go upstairs or they'd wake the baby. They couldn't go downstairs because the little girls were there. Dad was in the study, and Mom was watching TV in the living room. And they sure couldn't go out on the deck or they'd freeze. Suddenly Hannah laughed.

"What's so funny?" Roxie asked as she sat at the table.

"I was kind of feeling sorry for myself because of my big family. Then I realized how glad I am to have my family and to live in this big house. Think of the people who don't have a house or a family."

Her face serious, Chelsea leaned against the counter. "I knew a man in Oklahoma who lived in an A-shaped pig house. He had a twin-size bed and a tiny table with one chair in it. He cooked outdoors on a propane gas grill. He had to get drinking water from his nearest neighbor, and he took a bath in a stream. He didn't have a family at all. Not anybody."

"That's awful!" Hannah's eyes filled with tears.

"I'd rather live in a pig house than a cardboard box in a city," Roxie said with a catch in her voice. "I'm glad I live where I do. And I'm glad for my family, even if Lacy makes me mad sometimes."

The Best Friends were quiet a long time. A faint sound of music drifted in from the living room. The refrigerator clicked on, and the hum seemed extra-loud.

Chelsea sat at the table. "Hannah, did your dad tell you the name of a family we can buy Christmas gifts for?"

Hannah nodded as she pulled a paper from beneath some butterfly magnets on the refrigerator. "Elinore and Russ Beacon. They have six kids—two boys and four girls."

"I talked to Melinda Conners a while ago and told her what we're doing," Chelsea said. "She wants to help buy gifts for them."

"That's great!" Roxie laughed in delight. "I love seeing the change in Melinda. We'll take her with us to buy the presents. She'll like that."

Chelsea and Hannah agreed.

"Where does the Beacon family live?" Chelsea asked.

"In the really bad part of town." Hannah leaned her elbows on the table as she told them the name of the street and what the house looked like. "Dad drove me past there yesterday after we finished decorating the trees at the Conners home." Hannah shivered. "I'd hate to live that way! I can't believe I was feeling sorry for myself because of this family and this house! How really really terrible of me!"

Chelsea nodded. "I sometimes do the same thing. I think we should make an agreement to remind each other how blessed we are when we start feeling sorry for ourselves."

"I agree." Roxie nodded. "You'll probably have to remind me more than any of you. I *always* feel sorry for myself!"

They talked a while longer, then wrote a list of possible gifts and what they'd cost.

Chelsea looked up from the list. "You know, maybe the others in *King's Kids* would want to help buy gifts for the Beacon family too. Who votes we ask them?"

Hannah and Roxie laughed as they both voted yes.

Hannah tapped Chelsea's arm. "You always have a meeting, don't you?"

Chelsea grinned. "I guess so. What can I say? That's the way I am."

"I like you just the way you are," Hannah said, smiling. She knew how terrible it was not to have a friend. That's why she was willing to help Lena find a friend.

After more talk and more lists Chelsea and Roxie said good night and left. Hannah walked slowly to the kitchen for a glass of juice.

A few minutes after the Best Friends left, the doorbell rang again. Thinking one of the girls had forgotten something, Hannah ran to answer the door. She opened it wide, then gasped. Clint Jarman and Ira Griffin stood there. She couldn't get a single word out of her dry mouth.

Mr. Jarman smiled. He wore a gray suit and a white shirt. He looked different than he did in class. "May we come in?"

"Oh yes!" Hannah stepped aside so they could enter. Was she dreaming? Would she wake up to find herself in bed?

Smiling, Ira Griffin pulled off his hat. His eyes looked sad behind his glasses. "I told Clint how you helped me today."

Hannah felt weak all over. "I wish I could do

more." She started to turn away. "Come in and meet my family."

"We only have a minute," Mr. Jarman said. "I'm taking Ira to the airport."

Hannah's heart sank. "And I didn't get to hear you talk!"

"That's why I wanted to see you." Ira Griffin took her hand. "I wanted to thank you again." He took a deep, unsteady breath. "I must find my daughter and talk to her. I haven't been able to track her down, so I'm flying to Boston where she lives. I must find her and learn the truth. If I do indeed have a granddaughter, I want to know her. I want to make sure she's not in danger because of me. You understand, don't you?"

Hannah nodded, though she didn't understand how a man could lose track of his daughter and never know he had a granddaughter. "I'll be praying for you."

"Thank you."

"I'll see you in class tomorrow, Hannah." Mr. Jarman smiled.

Her pulse leaping, Hannah nodded.

Ira Griffin squeezed Hannah's shoulder. "Thank you again for your help."

"Thanks for coming," Hannah said breathlessly.

The men said good-bye and walked out. Hannah held the door open until they drove away.

The red taillights finally disappeared from sight. She closed the door and leaned against it. Ira Griffin and Clint Jarman had come to see her! She took a deep breath and slowly let it out.

10

The Rescue

On Monday afternoon Hannah stepped into art class and looked for Penny. The room was full of students, but Penny wasn't at her easel. Hannah bit her lip. Maybe Penny was in the lounge or restroom waiting for her. She watched Mr. Jarman talking to the Chinese woman. Hannah took a step toward them, then hesitated. There was no need to tell Mr. Jarman she was going to look for Penny. She'd hurry to the lounge and the restroom and still be back in time for class.

Just as she stepped into the warm hall, she gasped and clutched her bag. The man who had been following Penny was walking toward her! Was she in danger?

He stopped at Hannah's side. "I'm looking for Penny Graham. Have you seen her?"

Her nerves tight, Hannah shook her head. "Why have you been following Penny?"

"That's my affair," the man said sharply.

Hannah looked the man squarely in the eye. "I think I should report you to the head of security."

The man shook his head. "No need."

"Why are you watching her?"

"I can explain."

Hannah glanced around to see if there was help nearby in case the man was dangerous.

The man lowered his voice. "I'm Allen Smith, head of special security while the Griffin is here. I didn't mean to frighten Penny." He showed her his identification badge while he talked.

"How'd you know her name?"

"She's Penny Graham, and she's staying with her uncle, Royce Graham." Allen Smith rubbed a hand across his jaw. "When we learned the Griffin would be here and that Royce Graham lived nearby, we got nervous. Graham has a bad reputation, I'm sorry to say."

Hannah gasped. Did Royce Graham mean to hurt Penny after all?

"When she enrolled for the classes, we got very suspicious. We thought she might be an inside contact for her uncle to steal the painting. But it seems we were wrong. He hasn't made an attempt to steal it at all. I'm afraid we frightened her needlessly. But you must realize, we had to take every precaution."

Hannah nodded and forced back the panic she felt. "I tried to talk to Penny on the phone last night, but her uncle said she wasn't there. We stopped at the house, and he said she still wasn't there."

"We'll keep an eye on him. You don't have to be concerned at all." Allen Smith smiled. "We'll make sure Royce Graham or his wife don't get near the Griffin."

"What if Penny's in danger?"

"Don't concern yourself. We'll take care of her." Allen Smith excused himself and walked away.

Her head spinning with what she'd learned, Hannah stood quietly in the hallway. Voices drifted out from the classrooms. Smells of paints and cleaners wafted down the hall. She had to find Penny and help her! Penny probably didn't know her uncle might try to steal the Griffin.

Hannah peeked inside the classroom. Mr. Jarman was talking about value and negative space. Hannah sighed heavily. If she left, she wouldn't get to see or listen to Mr. Jarman. But she had to help Penny!

Reluctantly Hannah slipped on her winter jacket and hurried outdoors. The sun was shining brightly, and the wind wasn't blowing, so she felt warm. The parking lot was empty compared to Sunday afternoon.

Flipping back her ponytail, Hannah ran all the way to Penny's house. The neighborhood looked deserted. Wood smoke drifted from the chimney of the house across the street. Trembling, Hannah knocked on Penny's front door, but there was no answer. She walked around and knocked on the back door, but still there was no answer. She peeked through the garage windows. It was empty. Should she run back to school? There was still time to see Mr. Jarman. He might tell her again that she was beautiful. She shivered with pleasure, then frowned. What was she thinking? She wasn't going to think about being in love with Mr. Jarman! She was here to help Penny.

Hannah stopped on the front sidewalk and looked at the one-story, white frame house. The lawn was small and well cared for. Bare bushes stood close to the house. She couldn't walk away without investigating thoroughly—she just couldn't. She walked around the far side of the house and studied each window. She caught movement at one. Someone was inside! Was it Penny? If so, why hadn't she answered the door?

Hannah took a deep breath, walked close to the window, and daringly knocked on it. Wouldn't she be embarrassed if a stranger looked out? She felt like running away, but she forced herself to stay.

The curtain parted, and Penny peered out!

Hannah's heart leaped. "Penny!"

Penny cried out in happy surprise. She banged against the frame. "The window's nailed shut!" she shouted.

"Answer the door!" Hannah jabbed her finger

toward the door to try to make herself understood. "Open the door!"

Penny shook her head and wiped at her tears. "I'm locked in! Locked in!"

Hannah gasped, her hand over her heart. Had she heard right? "I'll try to get you out," she called.

"Hurry! Please!" Icy shivers ran up and down Penny's spine. Uncle Royce and Aunt Peg could be back any minute.

Her blood roaring in her ears, Hannah raced to the front door and hunted for a key. She couldn't find one. Her family kept a spare key in the planter near their front door. She thought maybe the Grahams did too. But she couldn't find a planter or anywhere else where they'd hidden a key. She ran to the back door and looked around. There was no planter, but there was a rock. Hannah moved it but found only bare dirt. In desperation she lifted the mat. Her eyes popped open. A silver key lay there! She grabbed it up and quickly unlocked the back door. She stuck the key back under the mat, then slipped inside the warm house.

"Penny!" Hannah shouted as she ran through the kitchen and into the living room.

Penny pounded on her door. "I'm here! In my bedroom!"

Hannah ran to the door, saw the key still in the lock, turned it quickly, and opened the door.

Penny leaped out, grabbed Hannah, and clung

to her. "I was so scared! I didn't think anyone would ever find me!"

Blinking away tears, Hannah patted Penny's back. "You're all right now." Her voice broke. "You're free."

Penny brushed at her eyes. "I . . . I prayed for help, and God sent you!"

"I'm glad."

Penny ran to the living room window and looked out. "We have to get away before my aunt and uncle come back." Penny started toward the door, then stopped. "Wait! I have to get Daddy's itinerary so I can call him."

"We can't take time for that. Grab your coat quickly."

Penny flung her arms wide. "I have to call Daddy!"

"Not now! We'll think of something. Come on!"

Penny grabbed her jacket and ran out the front door with Hannah.

A car screeched to a stop, and Penny screamed, "It's my uncle!"

Hannah looked frantically around, grabbed Penny's hand, and raced around the house and into the neighbor's yard. She heard shouting and knew Penny's uncle was following them. Hannah ducked around some bushes, then spotted a UPS truck parked at the curb. The door was open and the engine running. She pulled Penny over to it, and they slipped inside and ducked behind the driver's seat.

A few minutes later the driver climbed in and drove away. After a block Hannah lifted her head.

"Could you let us off here?"

The driver sputtered in shock. He pulled to the curb and stared at the girls. "What game are you two playing?"

"We had to get away," Penny said.

"We're sorry for hiding in your truck, but we couldn't help it." Hannah jumped to the ground, and Penny followed her. They ran the rest of the way to the art academy.

Hannah led Penny into the empty lounge. "Now tell me, why were you locked in?"

"I don't know! My uncle is trying to hurt my dad through me." Penny shivered even with her jacket on. "He'll look here first."

"Isn't there anyone who knows how to reach your mom and dad?"

Penny shook her head. "My dad only has his brother Royce. My mom won't talk about her family. She said someday she'd tell me about them."

"Does your mom or dad have a secretary?"

Penny's eyes widened. "Yes! Dad has Bob Pole."

"Call him!"

"Why didn't I think of him before?" Penny's face fell. "I just remembered . . . He's on vacation, and I don't know how to reach him." She brushed a tear off her cheek. "It's hopeless."

"We won't give up!" Hannah squeezed Penny's hand. "You can stay at my house until you can call your folks."

"Are you sure?"

Hannah nodded. "We always help others." She peered out the door. "We'll have to stay out of sight until Mrs. Shoulders is ready to take us home."

"I know Uncle Royce will come looking for me." Penny shivered.

"He will, but we'll stay out of sight." Hannah told Penny about Allen Smith and what he'd told her. "Mr. Smith will help us if we need it."

"And I thought he was out to hurt me! I sure was wrong."

Hannah smiled reassuringly. "Let's watch for Mrs. Shoulders. We'll make sure your uncle doesn't see us and follow us home."

"That would be terrible!"

Her nerves tight, Hannah nodded.

11

Shopping

Hannah peeked out the lounge door for what seemed like the hundredth time. Mrs. Shoulders had never been late before. Had something happened? Penny was staying out of sight in case her aunt and uncle came.

"I'm really scared," Penny whispered.

"God is with us." Hannah smiled encouragingly. She turned away from Penny and once again looked out the door. Fear pricked her skin like a million sharp needles all over her body—Penny's aunt and uncle were just walking in the door. Her face white, Hannah stepped back. "It's your uncle," she hissed urgently. "Quick, hide!"

Penny frantically dove behind the sofa she'd hid behind before. Dust tickled her nose, and she clamped her hand over her mouth and nose so she wouldn't sneeze. Would Uncle Royce find her this time? Would he take her back and lock her up again? A whimper rose in her throat, but she wouldn't let it out.

Hannah wanted to hide behind the sofa with Penny, but she didn't dare. She had to act like nothing was wrong. If Penny's uncle saw her, would he recognize her? She couldn't just stand in the lounge. If he knew who she was, he'd find Penny.

Grabbing her bag and her jacket from a nearby chair, Hannah took a deep, steadying breath and walked out of the lounge. Shivers ran up and down her spine. She pretended not to notice Royce and Peg Graham standing in the hall talking to three women. She tried to walk slow and steady, even though she wanted to run for her life. She heard Royce ask about Penny. Hannah wanted to look back over her shoulder and listen for the answer, but she kept walking. She must not stop or look back at the lounge!

"Hannah!"

She froze. She knew it was Mrs. Shoulders calling to her, but she was afraid to turn. Royce was sure to recognize her name. Hannah wanted to dash down the hall and out of sight, but she slowly turned toward Roxie's mom. Royce was looking right at her. Her body felt like soggy cereal. If she crumpled to the floor, Royce would really get suspicious. She stiffened her spine, forced her legs to move, and walked right up to Mrs. Shoulders. "Hi," Hannah said in as normal a voice as she could produce.

"I'm sorry I'm late," Mrs. Shoulders said with a wide smile. She looked warm in her calf-length green wool coat. "Ready to go?"

Hannah hesitated. What could she say? She wasn't ready! She couldn't leave Penny there. But how could she get Penny past her uncle? Silently Hannah prayed for help. There had to be an answer, but on her own she didn't know what it was. Still, she knew God would help her.

"Hold it right there, girl!" Scowling, Royce stepped up to Hannah. "I know you! You came to my house last night looking for my niece. You might even be the one who was with her a while ago."

Mrs. Shoulders circled Hannah's waist with her arm. "Sir, please don't frighten Hannah."

Royce frowned fiercely. "I want to talk to her!"

"She knows where our niece is," Peg said in a soft, nervous voice.

Mrs. Shoulders looked questioningly at Hannah. "Can you help these people?"

"No," Hannah whispered.

Mrs. Shoulders urged Hannah forward. "She's going with me now. Please, let us go."

Hannah pressed close to Mrs. Shoulders.

Royce growled something, caught his wife's arm, and half-dragged her down the hall toward the classrooms. The people they'd been talking to watched them for a minute, then hurried out the door.

Hannah pulled away from Mrs. Shoulders. "I can't leave yet," Hannah whispered. She watched until Royce and Peg disappeared into a classroom. Hannah turned to Mrs. Shoulders. "The girl you took home the other day is going home with me. I'll get her."

Mrs. Shoulders studied Hannah closely. "Is something wrong?"

"I'll explain later."

Mrs. Shoulders frowned thoughtfully. "I'll pull the car up by the door."

"Thank you!" With her heart in her mouth, Hannah ran to the lounge. "Penny, hurry! We have to get away right now!"

Penny crawled out from behind the sofa, dragging her bag with her. "What's wrong?"

"Your uncle and aunt are here in the academy. . . Hurry!"

Penny felt too weak to move. "What'll I do? . . . What'll I do?"

Hannah caught her arm and pulled. "Come on!"

"I'm so scared," Penny whispered through a tight throat.

"I know, but you have to come anyway." Hannah pulled again, and Penny finally ran out of the lounge with her. They ran outdoors and across the sidewalk to Mrs. Shoulders's car. Hannah pushed Penny onto the backseat. "Lay down and hide," Hannah hissed.

Laying her bag on the floor, Penny curled up on the seat. Her terrified heart pounded in her ears. Was she going to get away safely?

Hannah slipped onto the front passenger seat and closed the door. "Quick, drive away!"

Mrs. Shoulders looked in alarm at Hannah. "What's going on here?"

"That man's after Penny. We have to get her away before he hurts her. She has to call her dad and mom."

Mrs. Shoulders hesitated. "If you're sure . . ."

"I am. You can talk to my mom and dad when we get home. They'll tell you it's all right for me to take Penny home." Hannah frantically looked out the window to see if Royce and Peg were coming out of the academy. They weren't, but she knew they could anytime. "Please, can we go?"

Her cheeks bright pink, Mrs. Shoulders nodded and drove out of the parking lot.

Hannah watched out the back window. When they were a few blocks from the academy she said, "You can sit up now, Penny. It's safe."

Penny sighed in relief and sat up. She looked out of the window, making sure Uncle Royce's car wasn't in sight. She didn't see it, and finally she breathed easier.

At the Ravines Hannah thanked Mrs. Shoulders

for the ride, and then she and Penny hurried inside. The house smelled like baked beans and freshly baked bread.

"You're really safe, Penny." Hannah smiled as she took Penny's jacket and hung it in the closet.

Penny leaned weakly against the wall. "I was so scared!"

"But you're safe now."

"I don't think he followed us. Do you?"

Hannah shook her head. "You're safe now, Penny. We'll call your dad, and he'll tell us what to do."

"I hope we can find a number where we can reach him." Penny shivered.

"We will." Hannah patted Penny's arm. "Come meet my family."

Penny took a deep breath and nodded.

Later, after dinner, Hannah sat on the living room floor while her mom talked with Penny. Dad was upstairs talking care of baby Burke. The little girls were downstairs playing before bedtime. With a small sigh Hannah leaned back against the couch. She'd missed class today—she'd missed Mr. Jarman. But she'd been able to rescue Penny.

"I'm sorry we couldn't get in touch with your parents," Beryl Shigwam said as she patted Penny's hand. They'd finally tracked down a man in her dad's office who also had a copy of his itinerary.

"We did leave a message to have them call here. I hope it's soon."

"Me too." Penny flipped back her blonde hair. She liked Hannah's family. They were the first Native Americans she'd ever met. They were like . . . like real people. She should've known that before, but somehow she hadn't. She smiled wanly at Mrs. Shigwam. "I wish Daddy and Mom could come home, but I don't think they will. This is a very important mission for Daddy."

Beryl leaned forward with a smile. "Maybe your mom will fly home to be with you."

Penny hesitated a fraction of a second. "Maybe."

Hannah noticed Penny's hesitation. What was wrong between Penny and her mom? She'd ask later.

Just then the doorbell rang, and Hannah jumped up. "It's probably my friends." She'd told Penny all about the Best Friends. "Mr. McCrea is taking us shopping at the mall. He'll drop us off and pick us up later." Hannah had told Penny about the Beacon family and what they were planning to do. Chelsea had called to say Melinda was going with them. "Penny, do you want to go with us?"

Penny hesitated. "Will it be safe?"

"We'll all stay together. What can your uncle do even if he sees you?"

Beryl patted Penny's shoulder. "You're welcome to stay here with us."

Penny thought about it for a while and shook her head. "Thanks, but I'll go with Hannah."

"Good." Hannah smiled, and finally Penny did too.

Several minutes later Chelsea's dad dropped the girls off outside the mall. After he helped Melinda into her wheelchair he said, "I'll be back in two hours. Meet me right here."

"We will," the girls said. They looked at each other and giggled. They loved the freedom of walking through the mall by themselves.

Roxie and Chelsea held the doors open, and Melinda rolled on through. She smiled at them. "This is the very first time I've been here without Mom and Dad. It feels strange but nice."

The girls talked easily with Melinda, but Penny walked quietly at Hannah's side. Penny bit her lip. She didn't know how to act or what to say to Melinda. The others acted as if she were walking beside them, not rolling along in a wheelchair.

Roxie led the way to the toy store to find toys for the six Beacon kids. Chief Shigwam had told them their ages.

"They need clothes," Hannah said as they walked into the toy store. "But they need toys too, so we'll get both things for them."

Roxie nodded. "My mom says toys are as nec-

essary to kids as food and clothing." Roxie
shrugged. "Who knows why."

Kathy giggled. "I know I *hated* getting clothes
from my aunt when I was little. I wanted toys!"

Chelsea stopped near the stuffed animals.
"Once when I was five my aunt gave me a great big
gift wrapped in Santa Claus paper. I just knew it was
going to be a big doll—one I'd wanted forever. I
opened the box, and it was a blanket for my bed. A
blanket! I almost cried."

Kathy wrinkled her nose. "The worst gift I ever
got was some ugly pajamas from my grandma."

Melinda sighed heavily. "The worst I ever got
was a tennis racket last year."

The girls gasped.

"My aunt sent it. She'd forgotten about the
accident and that I was in a wheelchair." Melinda
brushed back her hair. "I cried for days."

Penny moved restlessly. She'd feel a lot better if
Melinda weren't with them.

"We'd better hurry," Chelsea said. She looked
at the list. "I'll get the truck for Randy. Hannah, you
want to get the model airplane for Drew?"

"Sure. Want to help me, Penny?"

She nodded. It was a relief to get away from
Melinda.

Almost two hours later Hannah walked tiredly
down the hall with Penny nearby. They were all carrying packages. They were headed back toward the

exit where they were to meet Mr. McCrea. Roxie and Chelsea led the way with Kathy several steps behind them. Hannah glanced around for Melinda. She was looking at some puppies in a pet store window.

Just then Royce Graham walked out of the store next to the pet store and headed right for Penny, an angry scowl on his face.

Hannah shouted, "Penny, run!"

Penny looked over her shoulder. "Uncle Royce . . ." she whispered fearfully. She tried to move but couldn't.

Melinda saw what was happening. In a flash she pushed the button on her wheelchair and rolled right at the man hurrying toward Penny. Melinda bumped into him, knocking him to the floor. Then she spun around him and rolled fast after the girls.

Hannah grabbed Penny and pulled her along with them. At the door Hannah looked back. Cara North was helping Royce Graham to his feet. Cara North and Royce Graham together . . . What did it mean? Was it a coincidence?

Her veins full of icy splinters, Hannah held the door wide for Melinda, then followed her out. They reached the door just as Mr. McCrea stopped his station wagon at the curb.

"Dad, Penny's uncle is after her!" Chelsea cried.

"Get in the car quickly!" Glenn McCrea lifted

Melinda in, folded her chair and set it in the back, then ran to the driver's seat.

Trembling, Hannah watched out the window. The only sounds in the station wagon were the hum of the heater and the rapid breathing of all of them.

Penny shivered and locked her hands in her lap as she waited for Uncle Royce to burst through the door and grab her before Mr. McCrea could drive away. But he pulled away from the curb and drove around the far side of the building before anyone walked out the door. Breathing a sigh of relief, Penny sank back against the seat and closed her eyes.

The others all started talking at once, while Hannah's head whirled with thoughts. Cara North and Royce Graham! Why had they been together? Hannah thought about what Cara North had angrily shouted at Ira Griffin. She'd said, "I know you have a daughter. And she has a daughter! I have a man working with me who hates your grand-daughter enough to do anything I ask." Hannah peeked at Penny. Could it be? . . . Was Penny Ira Griffin's granddaughter? But if she was, wouldn't she know it? Was Royce Graham the man working with Cara North? Somehow it all made sense, and somehow it didn't.

Hannah locked her suddenly icy hands in her lap. Had she uncovered the real reason Penny was in danger? Should she tell Penny what she suspected? Oh, she just couldn't! What if she were wrong? She'd wait until she knew the truth. In the meantime she'd keep Penny safe.

Glenn McCrea stopped at Melinda's house and lifted her back into her wheelchair. The lights from the Christmas tree in the yard brightened the front of the house. Lights twinkled from the tree at the living room window.

"Good night, girls," Melinda said gaily. "I had a great time. Penny, I'll be praying for you."

"Thanks." Penny smiled. "Thanks again for saving me. I'll come see you if I can."

"I'd like that." Melinda waved and rolled to her door with Glenn McCrea beside her.

Chelsea sighed loud and long. "We've had adventures before, but having Melinda knock over Penny's uncle was the most exciting and scary yet."

"I'm glad she helped me," Penny said softly. "I ignored her all the time we were shopping because she made me feel uncomfortable, and yet when I was in trouble she helped me. I guess she's a regular girl just like us."

Roxie told Penny about decorating the Conners family's Christmas trees and how they'd talked to Melinda and prayed with her. "She's happy because now she has hope in Jesus."

"That's just how I feel too!" Penny squeezed Hannah's hand. "Hannah, you've helped me to trust Jesus. Thank you!"

Hannah smiled. Would Penny be as happy when she learned the newest development?

Hannah looked out the window at the Christmas tree. But she wasn't seeing the tree—she was seeing Cara North and Royce Graham together. What would they try next?

12

Talking

Hannah slipped between the sheets beside Penny. Across the bedroom she heard the twins and Lena sleeping soundly. Sometimes Sherry moaned in her sleep. She did that if she was overtired.

"What a day," Penny whispered. She was wearing Hannah's warm pajamas. They were too short and too big around, but they were warm and clean. And she was safe in the Shigwam house where Uncle Royce couldn't get her.

Hannah stared up at the ceiling. The nightlight in the bathroom cast enough light to see shapes and shadows. The smell of bath oil wafted from the bathroom. Hannah turned her head on her pillow and said softly, "Tell me about your mom."

Penny sighed. "What can I say? She's my mom."

"You said she'd never tell you about her family." Hannah's stomach knotted. "Don't you know anything?"

"No. I just know she had a fight with them years ago. She won't talk about them or anything. She doesn't even have any pictures of them."

"Did you ask her why?"

"Yes, when I was little. One time when I asked, she got really mad and told me never to ask her again. So I didn't. But I sure wanted to!"

"It must seem very strange."

"It does."

Hannah yawned. "I guess we'd better get to sleep. I have to get up early."

"It'll seem funny to stay here instead of going to school. I do want to go to art class, though."

"It should be all right. You'll be with me. The security guards will be there. And Allen Smith too."

"They're taking the Griffin away Wednesday, aren't they?"

"Yes. I heard they're taking it to Detroit next."

Penny yawned and flipped onto her side. "Good night, Hannah."

"Good night." Hannah lay quietly a long time. She knew by Penny's even breathing that she was asleep. Hannah slipped out of bed. She couldn't stay quiet a minute longer with all the questions buzzing inside her head. She had to do something to help Penny, but what?

Maybe she should call Clint Jarman to see if he had Ira Griffin's phone number in Boston.

Her stomach fluttered. Was she thinking of calling because she wanted to hear Mr. Jarman's voice or because she wanted the information? "The information," she said softly, then smiled. That really was the reason! It felt good to know she could still care about Mr. Jarman without daydreaming about marrying him.

Hannah crept upstairs to the kitchen. The room was lit only by the streetlight shining in the window. Mom and Dad were already upstairs for the night. Since Burke had been born, they'd gone to bed early in order to get enough sleep. The past few weeks he'd been waking up at 5 to eat. They were trying to get him to wait until 7 at least.

Hannah pulled the phone book from the drawer and clicked on the light above the stove. She found Clint Jarman's number. Shivers ran over her. Could she really call him? Would he even give her Ira Griffin's phone number? She was just a kid. Why should Mr. Jarman even bother with her?

Moaning, Hannah closed the phone book and pushed it back into the drawer. Who was she kidding? She wasn't a detective—not even close to being one. Why'd she think she could solve this mystery?

She clicked off the light and slowly walked toward the kitchen door. She frowned. She couldn't just go back to bed without doing something. "Where's your courage, Hannah?" she whispered as she turned back.

In a snap she clicked on the light, pulled the phone book out of the drawer, found Mr. Jarman's number, and punched the numbers before she lost the tiny ounce of boldness she'd found.

A woman answered, and Hannah almost dropped the receiver. She'd forgotten Mr. Jarman was married. Besides, she'd expected Mr. Jarman himself to answer.

Hannah gripped the receiver. "Mr Jarman please."

"Who's calling?" The woman sounded impatient.

Hannah bit her lip. Should she hang up? She shook her head. "Hannah Shigwam . . . One of his students."

"It's late. Talk to him in class tomorrow."

"I can't wait that long. I need some information. I won't keep him long, I promise."

"This is Mrs. Jarman. Could I help?" she asked coldly.

Hannah twisted the phone cord. "I don't think so." Why didn't she hang up and forget the whole thing? No! She just couldn't! "I really do need to speak to him."

"Oh, all right!"

Hannah held her breath. She heard the phone

clatter and Mrs. Jarman shout for her husband. Hannah's face burned. Was she really such a big bother?

"Yes?" Mr. Jarman sounded impatient also.

Hannah trembled. "Mr. Jarman, it's Hannah Shigwam."

"Hannah! What a surprise. I'm afraid I thought it was going to be someone else. I'm sorry for being so abrupt. A couple of my students have been calling at all hours. What's up?"

Hannah leaned weakly against the counter. "I need to speak to Ira Griffin. I think I have information for him that'll he'll want immediately."

"What's this about, Hannah?"

She hesitated. "I'd better not say. But it is important . . . Honest."

Clint Jarman was silent for several seconds. Finally he said, "I trust you, Hannah. You have a level head on your shoulders. Do you have a pencil and paper ready?"

"Yes." She changed the phone to the other ear and poised the yellow pencil over the small pad. She wrote the number as he gave it, then repeated it to him.

"He's staying with friends. But it is rather late, you know."

"I know. I won't make a pest of myself, I promise."

"I'm sure you won't."

"Thanks for your help."

"By the way, Hannah, Penny Graham's uncle was asking about her today."

Hannah froze. "Oh?"

"He was frantic. I told him I hadn't seen her." He was quiet a while. "You weren't in class either."

"I'll be there tomorrow." She didn't want to tell him Penny was with her, but she couldn't lie to him either. She had to think of something to say to get his mind off Penny. Hannah's hand felt sweaty against the phone. "I hate missing class, especially since there are only a few more sessions left. You've been a really great teacher. Well, I have to go. Thanks for your help. Bye." She hung up before he could ask her about Penny.

Weakly Hannah sagged against the counter. She wanted to have the courage to call Ira Griffin, but she couldn't lift her arm or move her hand. But she had to call him! And she couldn't wait any longer.

"Help me, Heavenly Father," she whispered.

The strength returned to her arm, and she quickly pushed the numbers Mr. Jarman had given her. A man with a deep voice answered.

"May I speak with Mr. Griffin please? Tell him it's Hannah Shigwam from Middle Lake, Michigan."

"Hold on and I'll get him."

Hannah waited for what seemed like an entire year. Finally Ira Griffin said, "Hello."

She tried to speak, but her tongue felt numb, like after a visit to the dentist.

"What can I do for you, Hannah?"

The numbness left, and she said, "I think I know who your granddaughter is. I think Penny Graham is." Hannah quickly told Ira Griffin what she knew. "Is it possible?"

"I don't know!" He sounded ready to cry. "I haven't been able to get ahold of my daughter."

"Penny's dad is Jason Graham. I forgot to ask her mom's name. Is your daughter married to Jason Graham?"

"I don't know," he said hoarsely. "I lost track of her after our argument. She wasn't married at the time, and she said she was even going to change her name."

Hannah blinked back tears. It was hard to realize Ira Griffin could argue and get angry enough to lose contact with his daughter. "It could all be a coincidence, but it sure doesn't sound like it." Hannah twisted the phone cord around her finger. "Mr. Griffin, Penny's in danger. She's here with us right now, and we'll take care of her, but she needs her parents. And she needs you—if you are her grandfather."

"I'll do what I can. But please don't say anything to the girl until we know for sure."

"I won't. Good night, Mr. Griffin."

"Good night, Hannah. Thank you again for all your help."

She hung up and stood in the silence of the kitchen, her head spinning.

At a sound she turned toward the door. Looking sleepy, Lena stood there barefoot and wearing yellow pajamas.

"Lena! Why are you up?"

"I woke up, and I needed to talk to you. You weren't in bed, so I came to find you." Lena leaned against Hannah.

Hannah patted Lena's back. "Is something bothering you?"

Lena nodded. "It's Heather Robbins. She talks about herself all the time. How can we be best friends if she always talks about herself and won't let me or the twins talk about ourselves?"

"That's a big problem all right." Hannah led Lena to the table, and they sat down side by side. The house creaked. "Heather is an only child, and she's not used to sharing the attention."

"She really is selfish, Hannah. I picked up one of her activity books just to look at it, and she yelled at me to put it down. It really was embarrassing." Lena swallowed hard. "You know I wouldn't work a page in it unless I asked first."

"I know. You're a very thoughtful girl."

"So are the twins. But Heather isn't! I don't know if I want to be in a Best Friend Club with her."

"Sometimes it takes time to be a friend—especially a best friend." Hannah brushed Lena's hair off her cheek. "You remember how hard it was for Roxie to like me."

Lena nodded. "Because you're Odawa."

"Yes." Cousin Ginny had said it was important to say Odawa instead of the white man's word, Ottawa. Lena tried to remember to always use the correct word. Hannah didn't. She smiled at Lena. "But the more time Roxie and I spent together and the more we talked and got to know each other, the more we trusted each other. She finally realized I'm a regular girl just like she is, and I realized she was nice most of the time."

"Heather's sure not nice most of the time."

"You can help her learn to be."

Lena sighed. "I guess. But it'll be hard. She never gives me a chance to talk."

"When you're with her again, let her talk about herself. Even ask her questions about herself. Then you tell her something really short about yourself. Ask her something about herself, and then tell something really short about yourself again. Pretty soon she'll get curious about you and want to know more. Before you know it, you'll both be talking and you'll both be having fun. Tell the twins to do the same thing."

"It'll take so much time!"

"Being friends does take time."

Lena sighed heavily. "Hannah, I didn't know making friends was such hard work."

Hannah chuckled. "Let's get to bed so we don't fall asleep in school tomorrow."

A few minutes later Hannah tucked Lena into bed and kissed her good night. "God is always with you and will help you with Heather."

"I know," Lena whispered. "He did answer my prayer and give me best friends—Heather and the twins. I guess I never thought the twins could be sisters and best friends both."

"I'm glad you learned that. Sleep tight." Hannah walked silently across the room to her bed. Penny was tossing and turning and moaning in her sleep. Suddenly she sat bolt upright, her hand over her mouth, her eyes wide in alarm.

Hannah touched Penny. "What's wrong?"

"I had a terrible nightmare!" Penny shivered.

Hannah slipped onto the bed and sat beside Penny. "It was only a dream. You're safe right here with us."

Penny took a deep, ragged breath. "I dreamed I was hiding at the academy and Uncle Royce found me. He beat me and locked me in a dark room full of rats and snakes and spiders."

Chills ran up and down Hannah's spine, and she shivered. "That's awful!" What if Royce

Graham caught them both and did that? She pushed the thought aside. God was with them, and His angels were watching over them. Royce wasn't going to catch them and harm them! "It's not going to happen!" she said firmly, as much for her sake as Penny's.

"You're right." Penny lay back down and pulled the cover to her chin. "It was only a dream, and I am safe here. Not even Uncle Royce can harm me."

"That's right!" Smiling, Hannah dropped back on her pillow and pulled the cover up to her chin. "Good night again, Penny."

13

A Surprise Visitor

With Penny beside her, Hannah hesitated outside the academy. Snow swirled in the air. Christmas carols played over loudspeakers near the front door.

Penny clutched Hannah's arm. "What'll we do if Uncle Royce tries to grab us?"

Hannah shivered, but then she grinned. "We'll scream at the top of our lungs. The security would come running, and we'd be safe."

Nervously Penny pushed her long hair back. "Uncle Royce might convince them to let him take me."

"No way!"

"I should've stayed at your house," Penny whispered uneasily.

Hannah hoisted her bag onto her shoulder. "We'll go right to class like we planned. And after class we'll wait in the lounge if Mrs. Shoulders isn't here yet. Stop worrying."

Penny nodded. "I'm sorry, Hannah. I said I wouldn't be a coward, but I guess I am."

"No, you're not. You're just cautious. There's nothing wrong with that." Hannah held the door open for Penny, then followed her in. Warm air circled her. She smelled damp wool and coffee. She pulled off her jacket and hung it on the rack.

Penny hung hers, then turned toward the classroom. Her breath caught in her throat.

Hannah heard the gasp and looked around. Several students stood in the hall, but Royce Graham wasn't there. She saw Allen Smith, but she knew they didn't have to worry about him. He wore a dark suit, white shirt, and multicolored tie.

Frowning slightly, he hurried up to them. "Penny, I'm glad to see you're all right."

Her eyes wide, Penny backed away from him.

"It's all right," Hannah said close to Penny's ear. "He's Allen Smith, special security with the Griffin. I told you, remember?"

"Yes." Penny managed to smile and relax a little. "I guess I was afraid of the wrong person."

"You have nothing to fear from me." Allen Smith pushed back his suit coat and rested his hands on his hips. "How about your uncle? Do you know where he is?"

Hannah darted a look around. Was he waiting for them? Too bad for him if he was!

Penny shook her head. "Isn't he at home?"

"I've stopped by there a couple of times to question him, but he wasn't there. Let me know if you see him. I'll be in the hall when your class lets out." With a nod of his head Allen Smith strode away toward the auditorium.

Hannah smiled at Penny. "I'm glad that's settled. You don't have to worry about why he's following you. Now, let's get to class." Hannah hurried down the hall with Penny beside her.

Inside the noisy classroom Hannah smiled at Mr. Jarman, then pulled open the wide drawer that held her canvas. Smells of paint and thinner almost took her breath away. The earlier class had left a mess in the nearest sink, and she watched as one of the older students washed it down. Sunlight shone through the row of windows. The snow had stopped. Students chattered noisily as they set up their canvases and paints. Clint Jarman pulled away from two men talking to him and clicked on the bright overhead lights so that they cast the exact shadows he wanted on the still life the class had started painting after the last project was completed.

As Mr. Jarman called the class to order, Penny looked at her painting. She wanted to start all over again. Would she ever be as good as Ira Griffin? Why fool herself? She wasn't good enough to be in this class.

Hannah studied her work and groaned. It had seemed all right until she looked at it through the eyes of Ira Griffin. He'd probably tell her to quit trying. She picked up her brush and tried to do what Mr. Jarman was saying, but somehow it didn't work for her. Why couldn't she get the smooth glass jug to look like glass?

"Hello, Hannah."

She turned her head and gasped. Ira Griffin stood there with a plaid cap in his hand. He wore a gray sweater and black pants. "Mr. Griffin! You're here!"

"Yes. I'll talk to you later. Go to the lounge after class, will you?"

Feeling weak all over, she nodded.

Penny saw Mr. Griffin and smiled. Would she have a chance to talk to him again? What if he looked at her work and told her she didn't belong in this class?

Clint Jarman shook Ira Griffin's hand, then presented him to the class. "Class, it's our great pleasure to have Mr. Griffin here after all." Mr. Jarman turned to Ira Griffin. "Feel free to take over the class."

Mr. Griffin shook hands with Clint Jarman, then turned to the class. "Instead of giving a lecture, I'll walk around the room and answer any questions you may have about the work you're doing."

Hannah wanted to pinch herself to see if she were dreaming. Soon she'd have a chance to ask this great man a question! What could she ask? She had a million questions.

Mr. Griffin stepped up to a man in the first row. "How can I help you?"

"How can I get the shadow right?" the man asked.

Mr. Griffin answered, then walked to the next student.

Penny could barely sit still as she waited for him to get to her. She wanted to hide her canvas, but she kept working until he reached her. She wanted to smile at him and sound confident, but she couldn't. "I still have a lot to learn," she said in a tiny voice.

"But you have great talent." He smiled at her. "Keep on and you'll be famous someday."

Her heart leaped. She'd work until her fingers fell off!

He turned from her work and studied her face as intently as he had her canvas. Finally he walked away.

Hannah saw the look on his face and wondered if he'd learned the truth yet. Was Penny his granddaughter? What would Penny do if she were? Hannah smiled. That would be a great honor.

Mr. Griffin finally stopped beside Hannah. He rested his hand lightly on her shoulder. "Fine work," he said.

She flushed painfully as he looked at her glass jug. "I can't get it right. What should I do?"

He squeezed her shoulder and smiled. "Stop thinking glass, and stop worrying about glass. Think shape and value and color. The reflection of the light on the jug has its own shape and its own value in relation to all the other values you see, and it has its own color. You have the outline drawing of the shape; now match its color and value. Blend the edges, and add the highlights. After that you can think glass, and you'll see glass." He bent down to her. "Do you understand?"

She nodded. "I think so. Thank you!"

"And thank you for praying for me."

Tears sparkled in her eyes. "You're welcome." Her hand shook so much, she couldn't hold her brush. She'd have to put his advice to work later when her hand was steady again. She watched him walk from student to student. Toward the end of classtime he said good-bye, picked up his cap, and walked out. The classroom was so quiet, Hannah could hear the Christmas carols coming over the loudspeakers in the hallway. She felt sooo happy! The great Ira Griffin had given her help with her art!

After class the students all talked at once as they swarmed out of the room. Silently Hannah walked slowly beside Penny toward the lounge.

"He actually talked to me," Penny said in awe. "He said I have talent!"

Hannah wanted to tell Penny she might be Ira Griffin's granddaughter. With every bit of willpower in her, Hannah forced back the excited words. "He helped me get the glass jug right."

Penny stopped right in the middle of the hall, with students swarming around them. "Hannah, did you notice how he looked at me?"

She had, but she couldn't very well admit it. "How did he look at you?"

"Like he wondered if he knew me."

"Does he?"

"Ira Griffin? Of course not!" A wistful look crossed Penny's face. "It would be nice if he did, wouldn't it?"

Before Hannah could answer, Royce Graham leaped out from behind a tall man and gripped Penny's arm.

"You're going with me," he growled.

Penny gasped. She wanted to jerk free, but she couldn't find the strength. Helplessly she turned her head to see Hannah.

Hannah's voice seemed locked inside her throat. Her head told her to scream, but she couldn't get out even a tiny whimper.

"You're going to be very sorry for running away from me." Royce pulled Penny so close, she could smell his coffee breath.

Penny saw the rage in his eyes and felt it in his grasp. Was her terrible nightmare going to come true after all? Then she remembered that God was with her and that His angels were watching over her. She didn't have to let Uncle Royce drag her away and make a prisoner out of her. "Let me go!" she cried. "Help! Somebody help me! He's kidnapping me!"

"Shut up!" Royce shook Penny hard. He looked at the people who'd turned to stare. "I'm her uncle. She belongs with me."

Hannah suddenly found her voice. "Mr. Smith!" she yelled at the top of her voice. He'd said he'd be in the hall after class. "Help us, Mr. Smith!"

From down the hall Allen Smith came running. Before Royce could move another step, Allen Smith blocked his way.

Allen Smith narrowed his eyes. "Let her go, Graham!"

"She's my responsibility!" Royce snarled.

"Let her go!"

Penny struggled and finally broke free. She ran to Hannah and gripped her friend's hand hard.

"You're safe again," Hannah whispered.

Royce swore and tried to push past Mr. Smith. "Out of my way! You have no right to detain me."

"I have every right. You're coming with me. I have already arranged for Cara North to talk to the FBI. They want to talk to you too." Allen Smith turned to Penny. "He and Cara North were working together to extort money from Ira Griffin. And they were considering stealing the Griffin on display here. But they failed. You're safe from both of them."

Penny trembled. She didn't *feel* safe. She felt victimized and all alone. Tears burned her eyes. "What'll I do now, Hannah?"

She smiled. "You'll lift your head high and square your shoulders. God is with you always!"

Penny brushed away her tears. "You're right." She watched Allen Smith force Uncle Royce down the hall. She was indeed free!

Hannah spoke up. "I'm to meet Mr. Griffin in the lounge. Come with me, will you?"

Penny's eyes lit up. "Sure, I'll come!"

Laughing softly, Hannah walked with Penny toward the lounge.

14

Another Surprise

With Penny right behind her, Hannah stepped into the lounge. She stopped short, and Penny bumped into her. Ira Griffin wasn't alone! He stood in the middle of the lounge talking to a woman dressed in a tailored red suit and red high-heeled shoes. She had long blonde hair and was tall and slender.

Penny gasped. "Mother?"

Hannah stared at the woman. This was Penny's mother?

She turned. "Penny!" The woman ran to Penny and pulled her close. "I'm so glad you're safe!"

Hannah sank weakly back against the wall. She'd wanted things to turn out right, but she'd never expected Penny's mother to come all the way from Europe. Hannah looked from Ira Griffin who was wiping his eyes with a big white hanky to Penny and her mother. God had answered beyond what she'd dreamed or hoped.

Finally Penny turned to Hannah. Penny's eyes shone, and tears dampened her cheeks. "This is my mom, Marcia Graham. Mother, this is my friend, Hannah Shigwam. She practically saved my life."

Marcia Graham smiled at Hannah. "Thank you."

"You're welcome." Hannah flushed. Was that weak voice really hers?

"Mother?" Penny looked uncertainly from her mother to Ira Griffin. "I didn't know you knew Ira Griffin."

Marcia reddened. "I always told you I'd tell you about my family someday. Well, today is the day. Penny, this man is my father and your grandfather."

"What?" Penny cried.

Hannah walked weakly to a chair and sank to the edge. She'd been right! She'd put all the clues together and had solved the mystery!

Marcia Graham held her hand out to Ira Griffin. "Dad, this is your granddaughter, Penny Graham."

"Is it possible? I could see she resembled you, Marcia." Ira Griffin rested his hands on Penny's shoulders as he looked deep into her eyes. "My granddaughter," he whispered.

"I can't believe it." Penny's voice broke.

Ira Griffin slowly pulled Penny close against his

heart. "This is more than I ever hoped for. Thank God I found you."

Hannah brushed tears from her eyes. She didn't want to miss a single part of this meeting.

Smiling through her tears, Marcia Graham bent down to Hannah. "Thank you for helping Penny. We had no idea Royce was still angry or that he had such a diabolical plan. If we had known, we would have left her somewhere else."

"I was glad I could help," Hannah said.

"Why did Uncle Royce want to keep me if he hated Daddy so much?" Penny asked.

"Because of me," Ira Griffin said. He kept an arm around Penny. "My agent's assistant, Cara North, learned about you when she was trying to find a way to get me to keep on with my work. She contacted Royce, and because he was still angry with your dad, they cooked up this scheme. They knew that when I learned about you and knew you were in danger I'd agree to sign a new contract with Cara as my agent."

"How awful!" Penny cried.

Hannah thought about the terrible woman who'd practically attacked Ira Griffin at his car. She was determined to make him do what she wanted.

Ira Griffin nodded. "But it was worse for you, Penny. Cara said she'd pay Royce a tidy sum if he'd keep you a prisoner until I met her demands."

Marcia Graham stroked Penny's hair. "I'm so sorry, honey. We had no idea this was going on."

"And I had no idea I had a granddaughter." Ira blinked away tears as he looked into Penny's face. "The first time I saw you, I said you looked like someone I knew. You have so much of your mother *and* your grandmother in you."

Penny frowned at her mother. "Why did you keep me from him?"

Marcia dabbed at her eyes with a tissue she removed from her red purse. "We had a fight years ago just after your grandma died. He didn't want me to tour Europe with a group of my friends, but I did it anyway."

"And I was stubborn and foolish and full of pride. I wouldn't let her back into my life after she returned." Ira Griffin cleared his throat. "First it was hard, then it got easy to push her to the back of my mind. I missed out on so much by doing that . . . I never knew the man she married, and I never knew about you."

Penny touched her grandfather's cheek with her fingertips. "You wouldn't really quit painting, would you?"

He nodded soberly. "I found fame and fortune, but without a family it was worthless to me. Now that I have you both in my life, I can work again. But not with Cara North! She will be in prison if I have anything to say about it."

"I wouldn't want you ever to quit painting," Penny said softly.

"I give you my word I won't." Ira Griffin kissed Penny's cheek. "I don't want you to ever quit either."

"I won't."

Ira Griffin took Hannah's hand. "You either, Hannah. You've helped us more than you'll ever know. Thank you. Keep on being your sweet self, and keep on with your art. You do have talent."

There was so much she wanted to say, but all she could squeeze out was, "Thank you."

He'd said she had talent! Hannah's heart almost burst with happiness. Wait until she told the Best Friends! They'd be glad for her—just as best friends were supposed to be.

You are invited to become a
Best Friends Member!

In becoming a member you'll receive a club membership card with your name on the front and a list of the Best Friends and their favorite Bible verses on the back along with a space for your favorite Scripture. You'll also receive a colorful, 2-inch, specially-made I'M A BEST FRIEND button and a write-up about the author, Hilda Stahl, with her autograph. As a bonus you'll get an occasional newsletter about the upcoming BEST FRIENDS books.

All you need to do is mail your NAME, ADDRESS (printed neatly, please), AGE and $3.00 (U. S. currency only) for postage and handling to:

BEST FRIENDS
P.O. Box 96
Freeport, MI 49325

WELCOME TO THE CLUB!

(Authorized by the author, Hilda Stahl)